Web of Everywhere

JOHN BRUNNER

NEW ENGLISH LIBRARY

TIMES MIRROR

First published in the USA by Bantam Books in 1974
© 1974 by Brunner Fact and Fiction Ltd

*

FIRST NEL PAPERBACK EDITION MARCH 1977

*

NEL Books are published by
New English Library Limited from Barnard's Inn, Holborn, London EC1N 2JR
Made and printed in Great Britain by Hunt Barnard Printing Ltd., Aylesbury, Bucks.

45003094 6

DEDICATION

To *Robert Silverberg*
who asked for this story
and had to take something else
when it grew up to be a novel instead of a novella
                                                    —JKHB

INTERFACE A

Theseus
Blinded by the dark
Followed Ariadne's clew of thread

Ariadne
Has ceased her spinning
And all doors lead to the Minotaur

    — MUSTAPHA SHARIF

Chapter 1

'Look out!'

Thinking, in that instant of chill due as much to the change from excitement to alarm as to the step they'd taken from sub-tropical to sub-arctic, how absurd it was to blurt those words to a blind man. But Mustapha was accustomed to his lack after – how long? Fifteen years, fifty? It was not something one inquired about.

He complied, tautening into that strange state of total attention which, Hans Dykstra had sometimes imagined, could truly halt the passage of his personal time, poise him an arm's length away from the world experienced by ordinary people while he took exhaustive unseeing stock of it.

That too made Hans shiver, despite his climatized suit.

And then he realized: of course! Cobwebs!

He forced himself to take a deep breath, and fear subsided as icy air seeped through his mask. There was no light here, except from the powerful hand-torch he had brought, and the very first thing he had seen when he arrived had been gray fluff-thickened strands barring the exit from the skelter.

Illegal it might be, but one did hear stories now and then about people who couldn't afford a privateer and rigged man-traps of their own devising. . . .

'I sense no one,' Mustapha said in a voice which was not quite tinged with complaint. The eagerness which drove him had nothing in common with his companion's – at least none which the latter could recognize. They were collaborators, but they were not and could not be partners. One might say, 'The enemy of my enemy . . . ' And be able to proceed no further with an explanation.

Never mind.

Hans uttered the necessary words, and into the fringe of the lamp beam instantly rose a brown hand child-chubby as Mustapha's face, groping greedily for the spider's fragile legacy.

'Wait, wait!' Hans implored, thrusting away the blue flower, the speedwell, which of course he had held up before him as he entered the skelter. He hastened through his regular protective charms in his mind, meantime using one hand to sweep the visible portion of the house with his lamp and keeping the other alert to punch a getaway code should someone turn out to be already in possession. Such caution was very likely superfluous; an assurance from Mustapha was worth a dozen instrument readings. But since neither the radiation-counter nor the bio-assay unit had beeped, the place was obviously habitable, and it had been long since one stopped to ask polite questions of strangers who showed up unannounced in a domestic skelter.

'Wait why?' Mustapha demanded querulously. 'Because you can see a warning sign?'

With a sigh Hans abandoned his mental formulae before completion. 'No,' was his gruff answer. 'Because when you touch the webs you'll break them, and I want to get them down on film first.'

He unslung his camera and flash to record the delicate tracery marred by thickening dust.

'Keep your hand out of shot,' he added, eye glued to the viewfinder. 'Want to get yourself braced?'

'They will not find your pictures until they're meant to, after you're dead. So at least you originally promised me.'

'I could be dead, but you could still be alive,' Hans grunted, and wound the film on. 'Good, two will be enough. Go ahead.'

8

Plump fingers, with the slyness of a stalking fox, moved in air and located a web-strand, traced along it musician-precise without breaking it; found another; broke both in a deliberate gesture and savored the sensation of contact. Hans had witnessed him performing similar marvels before, but this was the most amazing. To *stroke* the full length of that spider-silk and leave it intact until the moment of his decision to snap it: such abilities sometimes made Mustapha seem inhuman. Men rush in where angels . . .

But there was no room in his mind right now for reflection, only for reaction. This time, no doubt about it, Mustapha had done him proud. He'd guessed from the form of the code he had bought that it was exceptionally early, and had dared to hope it might lie in the first million. On site, he was immediately ready to believe they'd located one of the first hundred thousand . . . assuming that this was Scandinavia, and everything pointed to it. The air was certainly cold enough, and facing him across the living-zone were big windows, absolutely black, silent witnesses of a far-northern night.

'Oh, wow,' he said under his breath. The phrase was archaic, but English was not his mother tongue, and anyhow if someone had invented a better way to express delighted astonishment he hadn't heard about it. Under the obliterating dust that floor looked like natural wood parquet; draped with cobwebs, that might be an authentic Hille chair; weren't those shelves System Cado . . . ?

'It pleases you?' Mustapha murmured, his study of the webs complete. At once he had reverted to his regular manner: cool, detached, as though he were a machine programmed to acquire and analyze with maximum concentration all new data that presented themselves, to idle in face of any precedented situation. This was the ninth time he and Hans had come together to a lost home. How his companion obtained the codes to reach them, Hans had no idea and intended never to ask, for fear of being told that they were relying on some ancient 'little black book', rather than some burgled bank of computer records, or bribery of a technician at the Skelter Authority.

And the Arab went on, 'I apologize for being over-ready to touch the webs. But they are so rare now. I had

9

not felt one since boyhood. I had almost forgotten them. Curious! One would have expected spiders to be tough.'

Yes, perhaps, Hans thought. But infection had come out of Central America – a fungus, or some microscopic parasite – and something kept happening to their eggs. . . . Well, one would also, at one time, have imagined that humanity was tough.

Aloud he said, 'I think this strike is the best yet!'

Cozy in his suit, he drew down his mask and inhaled the harsh air with paradoxical enjoyment. It was cruel to the throat, but it tasted infinitely cleaner than what he had left minutes ago, tainted with the open-sewer stench of the Mediterranean and the collective halitosis of Valletta. The dust merely added spice to its tang.

Unencumbered with equipment, Mustapha had walked forward, out of range of the handlamp's beam, to stand on the level floor and turn, as though on a very slow-revolving potter's wheel, soaking in the nonvisual information the house could afford him. Once or twice he clapped loudly, cocking his head, mapping walls and doorways and furniture, sniffing the while, memorizing new scents.

Somewhat more slowly, and somewhat enviously (but to envy a man who had been blinded! Crazy!), Hans also emerged from the skelter, hung about with safety devices, camera, flashbar, bag of spare film, lamp, instruments. . . . It was all gear legitimately come by, but there was nothing legitimate about the use he was at present putting it to.

His profession was that of a recuperator, his duty to share out reclaimed resources around the world to those who were in greatest need of them, or who could exploit them for the general good. It wasn't the lure of strange places which had enticed him to take up his dangerous and unlawful hobby, for he was routinely instructed to go to every continent as and when a reclaimable cache was reported to the Economics Authority.

No, what fascinated him was the form and pattern of a dead age, in suspended animation now but being gnawed by time so rapidly that unless someone made a record of it less tenuous than memory could provide its relics would have to be reconstructed in ignorance by the archaeologists of the far future.

10

If there were any.

This particular skelter was indeed one of the very earliest, half a century old and amazingly bulky, as big as a car. He understood that in fact some car parts had been adapted for the first skelters, just as Remington included bits from sewing machines in their original typewriters. So old a model might be developing faults. The thing had delivered them here safely, but would it send them away again? Worst of all: would it take Mustapha away – leaving first, as always, with his own incomprehensible curiosity satisfied – and then maroon him, maroon Hans Dykstra?

For an instant he pictured himself trudging across the snowbound wastes of . . . What country was this, anyhow? Sweden, Norway, Finland? Most likely Sweden; there was a Volvo plate on the skelter's crystal-box, rimmed with frost but legible. An almost vacant land, then. The winter population of Sweden was reputed to be down around two or three thousand now, mostly eccentric recluses, so hunting on foot for help in getting home would be absurd. In the summer, of course, things were different. There might be a million temporary residents by July.

He contemplated the skelter gloomily. Like most people nowadays – or rather, like most privileged people – he could undertake simple routine maintenance on his own model of skelter, the equivalent of changing a car-tire or a tap-washer, but he'd never seen a design this old before. If he were to start making inquiries about service manuals for obsolete Volvo skelters, though, within the day some bland official would track him down to ask what need he had for such data, and he had absolutely no desire to land a bracelet for code-breaking. No, he'd have to put his faith in the high standard of Swedish craftsmanship, take his chance of being disintegrated on the way to or from home, or of being stuck here until summer gave him the chance to mingle with a mass of visitors at a public skelter outlet.

It wouldn't be impossible to survive here for a while. It might even be fun, in a way. Novel, at any rate. He had never experienced such solitude as this lonely northern land promised. He had walked all around the living-zone by now, his heels on the hard parquet affording Mustapha the sonic

11

reflections he needed to build his chiropteran picture of their surroundings, and located the kitchen. Apart from the packs of food in the deep-freeze – which obviously he would not dare touch because they had been thawed and refrozen countless times – there was a huge store of canned goods. And if that wall-gauge were to be relied on, hadn't just jammed at a false reading, there were almost a thousand liters of oil in the heating tank.

On the other hand, Dany would report him missing at once, and they would promptly start turning the skelter system inside out in search of a fault which might have destroyed him in transit. There weren't so many human beings left that you could afford to have them disappear at random; the days when, if they heard about them, most people regarded a million deaths with equanimity, a mere garnish to breakfast, were over. And the last thing he wanted was to attract official notice. He'd just have to pray that the skelter would last out another dozen cycles.

By way of insurance, he retrieved his speedwell and placed it inconspicuously in a corner of the machine. That was a safe token to leave; its name had made the pretty little blue flower much the commonest of all life-symbols to take with you on a journey.

Then, pushing such considerations to the back of his mind, he photographed the living-zone, then the kitchen, then the sauna he discovered beyond, shooting to avoid the tread-marks which he and Mustapha had left in the dust as clear as in new snow.

Next he came to a small study, with an open bureau bearing a Halda typewriter, documents in pigeon-holes, a pile of dusty correspondence papers which he blew at gently until the name and address were legible. From it he learned that the house's owners had been called Eriksson, that they were indeed in Sweden, near a place called Umeå, which he would have to look up on a map when he got home, and something else which struck him as literally incredible.

Their skelter code was printed on the letterhead!

INTERFACE B

O my beloved I offer you my heart
To eat as you would bite a pomegranate –
  But beware.
A human heart holds seeds like a pomegranate
And some are sweet but more are poisonous –
  We have seen much death, you and I.

– MUSTAPHA SHARIF

Chapter 2

Almost, he snatched up the entire pile, thinking to dump it
on the big open hearth in the living-zone and set light to it.
He checked his hand an inch from the paper in the same
moment that he heard Mustapha's cool query: 'Hans, is
something wrong?'

'No, nothing,' he answered with an effort. True enough.
He had imagined something was, but that stemmed from
pure force of habit. Even if Mustapha was going to charge
him twenty thousand for the code which was here repeated
scores of times, he didn't need to fear the loss of his
monopoly. Years had gone by without anyone finding the
way – except Mustapha. Most likely as long again would
pass before other feet smutched this floor. Those numbers
were simply . . . numbers.

No, wait. They were something more, after all. A symbol,
a key symbol, of that strange far-off world of the recent past
which he was struggling to capture and preserve for posterity.
A good clear picture of the paper, or better yet an actual
sheet of it, would have to be included in his final report.

'You exclaimed,' Mustapha said obstinately. 'It must have

been for a cause. You have found a clue to the fate of the former occupants?'

A shadow of ghoulish hunger lay on his words, familiar to Hans from their previous expeditions together. (How *had* they managed to become open with each other, that first time? Hans had tried over and over to reconstruct the details in his memory, and been baffled of recall. He was sure of only one fact, that it had been Mustapha who broached the matter. Himself, he would not have dared. Nor, in a sense, had Mustapha 'dared'. He had determined that such trips could be undertaken in safety. There had been someone before, another man – or possibly a woman – who'd traveled with him to forgotten lonely homes, added those details necessary to comprehension of the whole which a visitor without sight could not provide for himself. But they had never spoken of the fate of Hans's predecessor.)

Curtly he explained, his head buzzing with plans for his later visits: the need for cleaning materials, floodlights, reference books about the culture of the country fifty years ago to explain the purpose of the mysterious gadgets such as he knew from experience he was bound to find, dictionaries to help him puzzle out a few of the letters and the shopping-list he had seen scrawled on a memo-board in the kitchen . . .

But when he came back he would be alone. For the moment, he owed Mustapha something more than the mere money which would by then have changed hands – in return, of course, for another volume of his poetry, hand-illuminated and magnificently calligraphed but to Hans totally incomprehensible. Regardless of the fact that he understood no Arabic, though, the frequent purchases he made from Mustapha to cover up the transfer of the large sums he shelled out for illegal skelter codes excited no remark. Little new beauty was being brought into the modern world, and what there was, was precious. A score of other people patronized Mustapha even more generously, and without ulterior motive.

Even Dany, who was resentful of the money her husband chose not to spend on her, had been impressed enough by the delicately illustrated books, lively with red and blue and

14

real gold-leaf, to believe that he was buying them as a safe investment for their old age.

Mustapha was talking. Hans compelled/composed himself to hear the words.

'There is a little smell of death, but it is so faint, it is more likely to issue, I think, from food which has rotted through several summers and been frozen again. Those documents: they say where we have come to. Do they also hint at what became of the people who lived here?'

Forgetful, Hans shook his head. Mustapha was looking at him directly and his eyes were bright in the lamp beam. It was not they which were at fault, but the nerves serving them. At first Hans had suspected that the poet was lying about being blind; he moved so surely about the room in which they'd met. Seeing eyes, inescapably one assumed that they saw.

Recovering almost at once, he said, 'No, but we can dismiss fallout, I think. This area must have been well out of range of the big blasts at Kiruna and Trondheim.'

Reflexively he confirmed that statement with a glance at his radiation-counter, even though it had remained silent. At most places he went to in the line of duty as a recuperator it beeped incessantly, and he had to sort through weathered industrial junk hampered as much by its distracting row as by his lead-impregnated suit.

'One would have expected that, yes,' Mustapha murmured. 'Disease, possibly? So many epidemics were imported here by the skelter . . . There are other rooms. For the sake of your "after" pictures, Hans, you go into them first.'

With an ironical little bow.

Sourly, Hans complied, mentally agreeing with the other's guesswork. Sickness after killing sickness had exploded like shrapnel from the few surviving reservoirs in less fortunate areas of the world into those whose inhabitants had neglected their immunization shots, as though they were convinced that they bore charmed lives. What, of the many that came this way, had carried off the Erikssons? Could it have been plague, diphtheria, cholera, rabies, smallpox – ?

No, none of these. Violence.

In the small room adjacent to the study a child's skeleton

15

lay in bed. The coverlet had been soaked with blood, urine and excrement, then with the liquid foulness of rotting flesh, and dried into a hard loathsome lump.

'Ah,' Mustapha said with the air of a man whose favorite suspicion has been confirmed. 'I take it we have stumbled on an actual body?'

Hans swallowed against nausea, though it was far from the first time he had chanced across similar horrors, and lowered the camera with which he had been ready to take one of what Mustapha scathingly referred to as his 'after' pictures. Customarily what he did at each of these lost homes was, as it were, to reverse the effects of time: record on his arrival the state to which the passage of years had reduced the place, then with much care and labor restore it to something like the way it must have looked when it was in regular occupation. 'Before and after', as the old advertisements used to say.

But a scene like this . . . No, he didn't want it included in his report.

Then, with that incredible depersonalized interest which at first Hans had privately termed callousness, but now knew was something his vocabulary furnished no name for, Mustapha slipped past, located the bed, ran his hands lightly over the disgusting mass until he located the shape of the skull.

'A child,' he said. 'Boy, girl?'

Hans surveyed the room, torch-beam dancing wildly on the irregular surfaces of a table, a half-open closet, a shelf of toys and books with brightly colored pictures. On a chair-back, casually deposited, two pathetic scraps of cloth, the parts of a bikini.

'Girl.'

'And young, by the size. Ten, twelve?'

'More likely ten. So far as I can guess from the toys and books without disturbing them.'

He thought in passing: funny, one had the impression that Swedes were casual about their bodies, that a child so young would be let run naked . . . but perhaps like so many other preconceptions it was a trick of perspective. Around the Mediterranean what had been believed about Swedes in the old days, fifty years ago, would logically have been based on the atypical behavior of expatriates.

A hall of distorting mirrors. The whole world had been turned into one – and sometimes the distortions had been mistakenly accepted for reality. It was going to be an infinitely long, infinitely painful task to set the consequences right.

'Perhaps in the adjacent room, then,' Mustapha said, 'we shall find traces of her parents. Lead the way again, if you please.'

There, in the master bedroom, two more skeletons, one sitting up in a twin bed, the other sprawled on the floor nearby, adherent to the ruin of an Icelandic pony rug. Among the shreds of dried ancient meat clinging to the ribs it could be seen that the latter's breastbone and one shoulderblade had been shattered. Also, on the wall behind, there was a pit such as might be made by a deformed and tumbling bullet.

Taking Hans's arm in a light grip, not to be tightened – and his fingers were dreadfully strong! – except if his companion tried to shake it off, Mustapha demanded a description in vivid detail before crossing the threshold, and at once began to compile an explanation.

'Ah, it comes clear. They were too casual with their skelter code, because in those days possession of a skelter was something to boast about. One midnight they were awakened by the arrival signal, and the intruder proved to be a thief –'

'Not a thief,' Hans cut in, dully pleased at being able to make the contradiction. 'A thief would have ransacked the house for money and valuables, left drawers and closets open everywhere. There's no more disorder than you'd expect in a lived-in home with a child around.'

'Someone who didn't come here to steal, then,' Mustapha accepted, unperturbed. 'But who wanted his presence kept secret albeit at the cost of three lives. A spy or saboteur – even a whole gang of saboteurs.'

'People playing skelter roulette?' Hans offered, hoping for a second chance to edit his companion's analysis.

'No, it's too recent a phenomenon. By the time that fad caught on they would have scrapped the notepaper with the code on it, perhaps if they were rich enough installed a privateer because it was about then that they started to come on the market. But I gathered that the skelter is an extremely old model?'

'Yes.'

'Very well, I believe in my saboteurs. Memory reports some kind of industry at Umeå; it was a city of moderate importance, a convincing target.'

He stood silent for a long moment, inhaling with nostrils flared, and then unexpectedly turned on his heel. Hans said, unconsciously rubbing the spot on his arm where those deceitfully gentle fingers had rested, 'You're leaving already?'

'Yes. Thank you for your assistance. I have what I came for. I wish you success in garnering what you came for, too.'

'When – when shall I see you again?'

'When I have something else to offer that's just as good.' With an enigmatic smile. 'Which may not be soon, but then this site should occupy you for quite a while, no? So I shan't hurry. Well, goodbye, and thanks again.'

There was a question Hans always wanted to ask at this moment of separation: whether he was Mustapha's sole customer for illegal codes. Now, once again, it tremored on his lips . . . but, once again, it remained unuttered. There was a faint wash of blue light from the skelter. He was alone.

Almost at once other thoughts were chased from Hans's mind by a surge of relief at being able to get ahead so quickly with his main task. The more he studied the house, the more convinced he became that, once restored to its pristine condition, it was going to be the star of his secret collection of words and pictures which – as Mustapha had reminded him – no one else must learn of until after his death.

Then, they would bless his foresight and dedication to the cause of history. If news of what he was doing leaked out while he was still alive, though, he would undoubtedly be braced, no matter how high-minded his motives. There were few absolutes left on Earth. The right to conceal a private skelter code had to be among them.

Well, now he could stop theorizing about the Erikssons' fate and get rid of their remains. Not before time, either.

Close on two-thirds of the planet's population had been killed by violence or disease within twenty years of the marketing of the first skelters; as though it felt chilly in the shadow of that tidal wave of death, men now were paranoid about the presence of corpses, and he was not immune.

Luckily, in the course of his regular work he had gained access to garbage-disposal codes which ensured delivery straight to the hot heart of a furnace. Presumably when the Erikssons were killed such codes had not existed, or the intruder would have bundled up the bodies along with the blood-stained bedding and rugs, made the beds afresh and left the house looking as though the owners had dropped down to the tropics for a few days and might return at any moment. Exactly as he planned to do now.

He felt fortunate that he didn't have to buy his garbage codes. They came expensive. They had to. They made it so easy to destroy the evidence of crime, especially murder.

He decided to attend to the chore right now instead of delaying it until his next visit. Used as he was to entering long-abandoned premises legitimately in the course of his profession – though never private homes, only factories and warehouses – and finding not two or three bodies but great piles of them, charred a little by pyres which other people had been too weak to keep alight until they themselves died, he found he hated the idea of coming back to this house that once must have been very beautiful and finding corpses in residence. It would make him feel too much like a trespasser.

He didn't bother to rehearse any prayers as he consigned the bodies to the skelter. In Northern Europe these people would presumably have been either atheist – in which case they wouldn't have cared – or Christian. As a moderately devout follower of the Way of Life he regarded Christianity with the same revulsion as black magic.

Let their evil Lord claim his own.

When the distasteful task was over he relaxed and spent a long while roaming from room to room in the house, everywhere finding new things to take pictures of, then disturb very delicately for fear time might have made them brittle, then, reassured, pick up and marvel at. To think

19

that this family, probably not exceptionally prosperous, had been able to buy and use, from new, objects that today would fetch a small fortune in the antiques market! He found a camera better and more costly than his own, a range of long-playing records in a well-sealed cabinet with a glass door any of which would attract bids from a hundred eager buyers, clothing of virtually imperishable synthetic fiber from which the dust fell away as he lifted it to reveal the brilliance of unfaded dyes, and more and still more whichever way he turned . . .

Abruptly he realized that his fingers and toes were growing numb despite his climatized garb, and his throat was stiffening, a sure sign of incipient frost-dehydration. There was, he remembered, a thermometer apparently in working order on the wall of the kitchen; when he consulted it, he discovered with alarm that he had been blithely wandering around at minus twenty Celsius.

Time for home. When he came back he must bring a heater.

INTERFACE C

This I am compelled to utter in another tongue
But it is a truth important enough to be spoken:
Some of those who call a journey-map a 'route'
Pronounce it 'root' and cannot tell the two apart;
Others say 'rout' which means 'to put to flight'
And oddly also 'to pull up by the roots' . . .
It is as though the genius of their language
Gave them warning in advance, which they ignored.

— MUSTAPHA SHARIF

Chapter 3

To possess two private skelters: it was not unheard-of. To own three: that was remarkable, but certain successful persons, mostly working for the planetary authorities, had attained that goal and shuttled back and forth between three homes.

To own three sited all in the same building, even though the building was large and sprawled into many shady colonnades, white-glittering domes, towers of marble and courts where lizards darted at the feet of priceless statues . . . That was unique. And their unique proprietor was the man who, some declared, was the greatest living poet: Mustapha Sharif.

But if anybody said as much in his hearing, he would wryly observe that there was very little competition nowadays.

Possession of his third skelter, high in a minaret where five times daily an elderly and arthritic muezzin came to call to prayer those of the local people who had not been seduced into following the infidel creed, the Way of Life, was not an achievement he advertised. The world might assume the existence of the first skelter; so famous a man was bound to have one at least. The lucky ones might even, by invitation, pass the privateer which guarded it and lavish on their host praise for the splendor of his home, which he could not see but always modestly said was worth maintaining for the pleasure it gave to others.

Equally, once having arrived whether by skelter or on foot or camel-back, visitors might guess at a second skelter. His estate was on rocky ill-favored ground, long unclaimed, but a skelter could and did bring in sweet water, delicate foods, relics salvaged from elsewhere on the planet.

But the third . . . Only two, out of all his many servants, were even aware that it was located behind that locked door on the last but one landing of a twisted staircase made of drab, worn tiles.

There was no light in the room, only a current of warm air from a high-set ventilator. He emerged into it, swiftly and deftly exchanged his climatized suit – necessary for the visit to Sweden – for his usual burnous and sandals, and after listening very carefully for the sound of footsteps unlocked the door, stepped out, re-locked it. The heat of Africa brushed him like fine wires, making his chill skin tingle.

On the point of turning downward on the staircase, he checked and changed his mind and instead took the last short flight up to the rooftop. He needed time to digest what he had learned.

There was a stool set out near the parapet. He felt for it, positioned it where he could lean comfortably forward, and faced the direction of ancient Luxor, which – so he had been told – was in line-of-sight from this tower. But he had scarcely begun to learn to think in pictures before he lost his vision. Instead he thought in terms of his other senses: the hot dry air bore him sounds that he readily identified, scents that he knew as intimately as his own hunger or thirst or fatigue. There were dates, camel-dung, humanity, cook-fires, growing crops, spices, wet cloth tentered on poles to bleach, and several other distinguishable aromas in the air today. The odors of life, not of death!

There was going to be another poem. He could feel the shy probing of its first tendrils at the back of his mind, those tender early shoots which eventually would knot and crack flagstones into fragments.

He toyed with a phrase or two. The images were elusive. It was too soon yet. But the time would come.

Content to wait, preferring not to wonder whether eventually someone might read and understand his work rather than simply admire it, and draw a correct conclusion about his inspiration, he turned his mind to another matter: Hans Dykstra.

He had made a mistake in choosing that man to go with him to the nine lost homes. There had better not be a tenth.

In the beginning, it had seemed that Hans would be an ideal companion. There were others who might have been equally eager to buy illegal disused codes, but they were greedy, like his own former partner . . . whom he had been compelled to lose, regretfully but with small compunction, when he started to pilfer items rare enough to be valuable in such quantities that the authorities grew suspicious and clamped down. He was buried, conferring the life of his body on a field of corn.

To come upon somebody who wanted to leave, as a personal bequest to the whole of mankind, a series of documented samples of the past, one typical family home from each major culture of the pre-skelter period, but was content to store up his reports until he was safely dead – yes, that had seemed like a tremendous stroke of luck.

But Mustapha was wise to the ways in which a man could change. He knew beyond any possible doubt that the idea of being famous in his life time was eroding Hans's original determination as surely as a river erodes the lip of a waterfall.

Sooner or later he would make a mistake. Sooner or later he would be tempted beyond endurance; he would carry home with him some precious object – more likely to be a tool, perhaps a camera, than a mere ornament – and it would be recognized by someone aware that Hans Dykstra was not entitled to possess it . . . There was a great deal left from the heyday of mankind's inventiveness, but not so much that it was impossible to figure out such things.

And when that moment came, there would be trouble.

23

Dreadful trouble. Therefore the moment had better not arrive at all.

More content after having reached that decision, Mustapha relaxed into pure enjoyment of the sounds and scents that the breeze bore to him. He was glad he had chosen to settle here in Middle Egypt; it was a place of strong vivid stimuli, its wind alive with grit from the deserts to the west, its sunshine harsh and its night air cold, its water flavored with the essence of inner Africa, and many, many of its rocks chased with inscriptions left by long-dead hands.

It was about time he went back to the Luxor ruins and refreshed his fingertip acquaintance with the statues and the stelae.

Establishing himself here had not been easy. There was much history in the area, both ancient and modern, with a great gap in between the two. First, a community had flourished and faded in Pharaonic times. Then, for a long while, nothing much happened; the life of a small village repeated and repeated itself. And then they built the Aswan High Dam – not the first, which did little damage, but the second newer dam – and stole away the annual floods from the peasants lower down and rendered millions of hectares down-river infertile, sterile, useless. Starving, whole villages of people had trudged south seeking new homes, and an exhausted few had given up the journey here where it was possible to raise subsistence crops and pasture a small herd of goats.

Later, when Cairo and Alexandria were bombed, the Aswan High Dam was destroyed too. Another horde of refugees, this time much larger, straggled along the banks of Father Nile, and found that this was as far as they need travel in search of regular floods and revitalizing deposits of silt. In a year there was a huge new town: too big for a village, built of too many shabby hovels to be called a city.

At first they were jealous of their well-watered land, and declined to offer strangers any welcome. But they were growing slowly more tolerant. Indeed, they were becoming proud that their neighbor in the handsome mansion, though not Egyptian by birth, was admired the world around, and was generous to the poor, and gave work to the deserving, and altogether behaved in a manner befitting those enjoying Allah's favor . . . bar one thing. He had truck with that instrument of Shaitan, the skelter. Even the most ignorant mud-grubbing *fellahin* were aware that the impiety of this invention had caused divine wrath to descend upon the world.

Their reservations, however, were being tempered by time. And by the judicious donation of good seed, new strong baby camels and donkeys, useful tools . . . Those could be cleansed of the smirch the skelter had left on them and put to honest use. Slowly he was winning the people over. Now, when he held open house on a feast-day and invited the local imams to preside at a night-long recitation of the Blessed Koran, many hundreds of the younger people came and sat in his courts.

A footstep on the stairs. Thinking he had mused so long, it was time for the muezzin to utter a prayer-call, he roused and turned.

But those soft slippers did not belong to the muezzin; here came Ali, his most trusted body-servant.

'What is it?' he demanded.

There were shushing sounds: the man was bowing.

'It is to be hoped that the work will not suffer,' he said in a tone of obsequious regret. 'One attends below, however, who wishes urgently to speak with you. His name is Dr Frederick Satamori.'

Mustapha's heart lurched halfway to his soles. The Deputy Director of the Skelter Authority! What could have brought him here, instead of putting in a phone call?

A myriad fearful images chased one another across his mind: memories of all the houses he had visited illegally, all the codes he had sold first to his former partner, then to Hans Dykstra who was so unconvincing in his rôle as a collector of finely-calligraphed books of Arabic poetry . . .

He gathered himself with an effort. 'Request Dr Satamori to make himself comfortable in the Room of the Leopards,' he directed. 'Bring him refreshments. Inform him that I shall join him in a few minutes.'

'The effendi's will is done,' Ali said, backing away with his sandals scraping the sand-dusted floor.

But it was more than a few minutes before Mustapha regained his normal composure and was able to find his way down the twisted staircase.

INTERFACE D

Time was when any lover, seeing his mistress
Was gone from the room, might call for her
And be assured that she would hear his cry.

O my beloved I do not treat you coldly.
Rather am I haunted by the knowledge
That one step may have put the world between us.

— MUSTAPHA SHARIF

Chapter 4

Hans wondered absently: what had the woman of that house been like? Tall, from her skeleton propped up in bed (devoid of a visible wound like her husband's but maybe she was stabbed in the throat or belly instead of shot) – but beautiful? Blonde? Blue-eyed?

Well, no doubt there would be pictures of her in an album or a drawer, and of her husband and child, even though none had been on display.

She must at all events have been better than that lazy greedy incompetent smug ungrateful . . .

Resentful thoughts in his resentful brain, he stepped out of the skelter into his own hallway – and Dany was rising from a chair to confront him.

He stopped, petrified. She had no business to be at home! She had told him she was off to a treasure-hunt party, a common and indeed a favorite gimmick in the circles she frequented, and he had relied on her solving the imbecilic clues, finding her way to the right place, staying at least several hours in the company of her friends.

Hers. Not his.

But here she was – and here he was, with the mask he'd

27

put on after her departure still around his neck, frost on the outlet vent of his suit, a score of fatal clues in plain sight for anyone to strand a noose for him!

Or worse: a bracelet, symbol of living death.

'Hans, where the hell have you been? I want your help!'

Words flared instantly into his consciousness: 'Liar! When you accept help the millennium will have arrived! I've told you over and over that you need it, and Karl Bonetti would supply it, and – the hell with you. May your next bug be fatal.'

But he couldn't say that because he was ashamed of even half-meaning it; he was hung up on a problem called 'conscience', very contra-survival for the individual inasmuch as it made him vulnerable, but enjoined on him by the faith he had adopted, the Way of Life. Besides, to have an actual wife, legally bound – no matter that she was aging, fat, plain, querulous and selfish – was a great status symbol, bringing young subordinates to him during brief breaks from the job in Caracas or Calcutta or Cardiff to pose problems to him about their love-lives and ask his experienced opinion. Thanks to contagious puerperal fever, CPF, men outnumbered women five to three, and the disease was still rife even in those underprivileged communities where desperation had turned the ancient preference for sons topsy-turvy and they were actually trying to breed for girls, which meant there was no surplus to be disposed of into the ranks of the skelter-traveling elite, and until sufficient vaccine to treat half a billion people all at one go could be deployed the pattern would remain constant: any female who was even passably attractive could and generally would ignore marriage, trading in one man for another because he was younger or had better prospects or simply because there had been a row the night before.

In any case, Dany was stupid, and would never put two and two together from his outfit, because she had so often seen him come home similarly clad from a day's work.

Nothing to be afraid of!

So get her out as fast as possible, which meant going to any lengths to avoid a quarrel. He said peaceably, invoking the authorized hobby which he had adopted as a cover for his real pastime, 'I've been out shooting photographs as

28

usual. What's the trouble, and what can I do?'

And looked at her for once, instead of merely registering her presence.

The sight was remarkable. She had on a pathetically glamorous new outfit, obviously expensive, hand-embroidered with huge flowers: Shapex leotards, Shapex bolero, wrinkled skin between, a tropical or sub-tropical style more extreme than was common around the Med in winter, tipped with hood, boots, and gauntlets lined with fur (genuine, as he well knew because his team had found skins during a survey they had lately mounted in Saskatchewan), and framed with an all-zones climatized coat currently wide open as though she were too desperate for time to take it off even in the temperate air of Malta. Not only her face, but her legs, bare midriff and presumably arms had been plastered with inexpert makeup; she jangled with jewelry and stank of far too much perfume. But so long as she was content with her appearance ...

'I've been invited to a party at Chaim Aleuker's!' she half-screamed, holding up a slip of card. 'But I can't figure out the clue in the invitation!'

Hans started in disbelief. Invited to a party by Chaim Aleuker? This – this *wreck*? Oh, it must be a hoax! Everybody knew that Aleuker was probably the richest man alive, thanks to having invented the privateer, the code-shifting device which changed the skelter from a wild beast to a domesticated draft-animal ... as it were. Millions of people who had never met him reacted to his name as to an electric shock, and Hans did so now.

For an instant he wondered whether he could be the one in the wrong, making ill-founded judgments. After six years of marriage, he was sharing little of his daily life with Dany. Perhaps she did possess some outstanding quality; perhaps the fact that she had stayed married to him had singled her out, or some other aspect of her personality had –

But she was disillusioning him already.

'Don't look at me like that!' she snapped. 'It's perfectly true. Apparently Aleuker is bored with the people he knows and wants to meet some new ones, so he's sent out cards like this all over the world. Molly Chu got one as well, but the bitch won't join forces to work out what it means!'

29

'You should consult the library computer,' Hans suggested, his tone still level and polite.

'Think I'm an idiot?' Dany blasted. 'Think I'd have asked you if the computer had been any help, you – you pompous sod?'

Alarm signal. Next she would be raking up his past, about which he was five years too old not to feel embarrassed even if living with Giuseppe and Hakim had been *faute de mieux*. Their quarrels always followed an identical pattern because they had not grown up in the atmosphere of tolerance displayed by the post-Blowup generation.

It must be great to have come to terms with reality instead of laboring under the delusive burden of a vanished world, leaden with prejudices and preconceptions. He did do his best, struggled to accept the doctrines of the Way of Life and act on them. Perhaps if he had managed to find a younger wife. – No, that was out of the question. Perhaps he ought to have resigned himself to never marrying, especially since the marriage was compulsorily childless . . . ?

Younger people had no memory of ancient evils like churches and nation-states. But they were all too keenly aware of their legacy.

Their frontiers nullified by the skelter, under constant attack by saboteurs and partisans who could be half a world away before their time-bombs exploded, five of the Great Powers had gone into insensate nuclear spasm as though they had taken strychnine. The survivors, or at least some of them, believed their governments had also been responsible for the subsequent epidemics. Given that foundation to build on, they had abandoned at last everything their ancestors took pride in: patriotism, religion, conformist morality, group solidarity . . . Oh, not completely, not all at once. But for the third and final time the wisdom chain had been shattered; so ran the teachings of the Way of Life.

In the beginning, the argument declared, to be older meant to be wiser – to have had more experience of how things are, to be more in touch with the reality of human existence.

Then came a war that murdered a whole generation of

fine young men in mud and blood, and murmurings of dissent accompanied them to their unmarked graves.

It was said, 'We have fought the War to End War.' Many believed, and were comforted.

In one more generation there was another war, that killed not only young men but old people and little children in their beds, that loosed the firepower of the universe on the fragile flesh of man.

By that time there were young people saying in tones of extreme puzzlement, 'Grandfather promised peace to father and father swore he would preserve it and father is dead in an ugly, cruel manner. Can we trust nobody at all?'

And there came the third war, the Blowup, and the wisdom-chain – already filed twice at its crucial link – snapped.

It was a new world. But a new world that must understand the old in order to surpass it. Hans Dykstra was convinced of that.

Right now there was no time for reflection, though. He needed some means to placate his wife. Being too slow, he failed. That was unusual. Ordinarily he was quick to react and forestall her; he had to be, because the risk of her leaving him was so high. No matter that she was close on fifty; no matter that under her thick face-powder dark bags marred her eyes and her cheeks were crested with blue-red broken veins; no matter that her bust, her belly and her bottom sagged – she was *a wife*, and for a young man nowadays no achievement surpassed stealing away a wife . . . unless it were abandoning her in her turn, a just act of punishment, as though CPF which had shrunk the proportion of females so low that many men had to resign themselves to never having a woman were in some way the fault of all women.

But this time Hans was laggard. She made it as far as sobs and wails.

She was eighteen years older than him. Like many of her generation, of both sexes, she was subject to crying fits born of sheer despair at the disappearance of the world she had been taught to believe in as a child. Perhaps earlier than the average she had learned to exploit tears as a weapon

31

against anybody who worried about her, who cared whether or not she killed herself in accordance with her frequent threats. It was there, Hans suspected, that one should seek the reason for her not accepting the invitation she had been granted by Karl Bonetti.

Karl was a psychiatrist who practiced on the neighboring island of Gozo. Islands were popular among those who were lucky enough to enjoy access to the skelter system; they were instant geographical symbols of freedom from the limits of separative space. This condition of depressive nostalgia being so common, he had literally hundreds of patients on supportive therapy because he couldn't cope individually with them. But Hans had located a drug Karl desperately needed dug out of the scrap-pile of Europe, and from gratitude he had offered to add Dany to his list.

One of these days Hans was going to *insist*. But not today. Right now he wanted her safely out of the way so that he could adjourn to his darkroom and see how the pictures of the Swedish house had come out.

'Let me look,' he cajoled, and the sobs switched off like a light and she gave him the card with the hopeful expression of a slum child promised a trip to the wonderland of the country. He selected the image with conscious pride from the stock of data about the near past which he carried in his head. In the old days it had been said that the period of history about which people knew least was the one directly before they were born: too recent to be taught from a book, too vivid still for their elders to offer an objective appraisal. He had resolved not to let that be true in his own case.

The card bore a short enigmatic verse, akin to a crossword-puzzle clue. That much he had expected. He had not foreseen that – if this did indeed emanate from Chaim Aleuker – it would be so childishly simple.

He read aloud, without stressing the rhythm, 'I'll give to you some exercise and syllogisms from the wise. Madam will you walk, madam will you talk, madam will you walk and talk with me?'

'It's – it's sort of like poetry, I think,' Dany ventured. 'The library computer says it goes to an old English tune called *The Keys of Canterbury*.'

'So I suppose Canterbury was the first place you made

32

for?' he countered – more scathingly than he had intended. The last thing he wanted was for her to lose her temper so completely she would abandon all hope of finding her way to the party and stay home for the pleasure of spoiling his own leisure-time.

She colored, although one would have imagined her too old to blush, and miraculously replied in a mutter instead of a scream.

'You can't. Not the original one, anyway. They dropped so many bombs on Eastern England. But there's another Canterbury in New Zealand, so I went there, but there wasn't anyone to give me the second card, and – '

'Oh, honestly!' He handed back the card. 'Athens! The Lyceum! Aristotle founded a school of philosophy there, and they called it the Peripatetic School – the walking-around school – because of his habit of strolling along while he was lecturing.'

'Are you sure?' she asked doubtfully.

'Ah . . . No! I'm not even sure the Lyceum still exists, even as a ruin. But I think it may; Athens was among the few capital cities that didn't get blasted, wasn't it? Look, you check out the idea, and if it doesn't fit come back and see if I've thought of an alternative.'

He had been ready to cap his contribution to her day's amusement with a kiss, but his embryo gesture went to waste. She snatched the card back and headed for the skelter at a near-run, tossing over her shoulder a word of thanks that was literally cut in half as the transmission effect displaced her.

Typical!

But at least she had left him in peace. For that small mercy he made perfunctory obeisance to the nearest life-symbol – here in the hallway they kept a tortoise, because Dany refused to be content with a mere plant in sight of the spot where invited guests gained their first impression of the 'Dykstra Residence' – before shutting his light-tight darkroom door.

3

INTERFACE E

Father!
You desired me to do you honor
As a dutiful and loving son.
Father!
I am indeed obliged to you because
It was you who facilitated my existence.
Father!
You must not imagine that I'm disrespectful
But the best way I can conceive to honor you,
Father,
Is to think otherwise and make different mistakes.

— MUSTAPHA SHARIF

Chapter 5

Dr Frederick Satamori hailed, of course, not from mainland Japan but from Okinawa (again, the association to the concept 'island'!); there were excellent reasons for that.

And their meeting was in the Room of the Leopards — leopards their owner had never seen, could scarcely imagine, for they existed in paint on the walls and had been varnished over so that not even the minuscule discontinuity between one color and another revealed the fine detail of the design to Mustapha's probing fingers.

Yet imagination populated the room with watchful threat: the alert tension belonging to beasts which must scent, spot, run down and overcome their prey. Sighted or blind, Mustapha who had early grown acquainted with the reality of such abstracts as 'hunger', well understood the concepts 'quest' and 'quarry'. To come in here was to taste blood in anticipation.

Yet he had no known grudge against Satamori. He might have picked the Room of Elephants, or of Fishes, or of Flowers . . .

Never mind. They were both here, and there was tea or coffee — the scents mingled — and Satamori had come fresh from a place that flavored his presence with jasmine, lavender and the smoke of some resinous tree being burned on an open fire.

And rose and clasped his host's proffered hand and spoke formal greetings that conveyed less information than the sweat of his palm.

This man, Mustapha thought, is frightened. So am I. But he, having eyes, is less likely to be aware of the fact.

Good!

Relaxing, he sat down and inquired, 'Fred, why bother to come calling in person when there was a risk of my discourteously making you wait? You should have phoned!'

'There are times,' Satamori said dryly, 'when waiting for a call to be put through makes one more impatient than waiting to be let past a privateer. Today is – '

'My servants made you wait in the skelter?' Mustapha interrupted in horror.

'No, no! They were the soul of courtesy! Indeed it was not my idea to disturb you, but Ali's; I was very happy to break my journey.'

'Break . . . ?'

'Why, yes. I have to go around the world today, to its other side. Switching from dawn to evening is no longer easy for me. I'm old.'

'That isn't true,' Mustapha said.

'You are kind, but I'm afraid it is. I'm still under sixty, but the strain is beginning to make me understand what old age is.' Satamori sighed loudly and took a sip of the coffee he had chosen from the range of available refreshments.

'And so,' he added after a pause, 'are too many of us.'

Mustapha waited.

'Anyway,' the visitor resumed, 'I felt it worth the risk of interrupting your contemplation and was quite content to hang about for an hour or two until Ali's patience was exhausted, thinking we might go on together to Chaim's party.'

'What party?'

Satamori almost dropped his cup. 'But – but surely of all people you must have been . . . ?' His voice trailed away.

'I begin to comprehend,' Mustapha said. 'Are you referring by any chance to a treasure-hunt party?'

35

'What else?'

'I see,' Mustapha murmured, and relished the conscious irony of the phrase. 'You too believe that by sprinkling the planet with clues that may come to the attention of random people, and which require a moderately advanced IQ to unravel, we can find the next generation of managers and administrators for Earth.'

'I – I can't conceive a better way,' Satamori granted. 'I shouldn't have mentioned the matter, though. I'm sorry. I simply was not aware that you were opposed to it.'

Mustapha leaned back, stretching cramped limbs. He said, 'It is not I who are opposed. It is something deeper, the force which evolved us.'

Brief blank silence. Satamori said eventually, 'You are adherent to the Way of Life? One had assumed that you must be – '

'Moslem because I chose to live in Egypt?' Mustapha cut in. 'Not at all; I am a skeptic. But I picked on Egypt because it was here that the cycle of the seasons, the rise and fall of the Nile, taught men to create absolutes: strict measures of distance, area, time elapsed . . . I often think of death. When I do, I feel certain I would rather die in the faith of the modern upstarts than in the faith of my ancestors. Has that notion never crossed your mind . . . ? Forgive me; it is not something one asks a friend. Being blind occasionally makes me tactless.'

'You . . . ' One could hear Satamori moistening his lips. 'You hold Moslem ceremonies here at your home.'

'Indeed, indeed. But as to the Koran – well, without wishing to appear arrogant, I could have compiled a more convincing book of divine revelation myself. The same goes for the Christian Bible, and the Little Red Book as well!' Mustapha laughed to diminish the weight of his words.

'And you could no doubt also have edited the doctrines of the Way of Life?' Satamori snapped.

'My dear friend, I did – I *did*!'

The silence was half-strangled. At long last Satamori forced out, 'If this is another of your subtle jokes, you must pardon a foreigner for not – '

'Ah, I am doing what I always do without being able to help myself!' Mustapha cried. 'When I'm interrupted during the composition of a poem – no, don't blame yourself, I was making very poor headway and the result will be all the better for being punctuated by a night's sleep – but when I *am* interrupted I tend to grow snappish. I've given offense without intention. Let me hear that I've apologized for it to your satisfaction!'

'No offense was taken,' Satamori muttered.

'Ah, I'm glad. But I did provoke you into suspecting me of a somewhat silly joke, did I not? I should erase that notion too. I meant what I said to be literal. I did edit many of the sayings of Prince Knud – from an English version admittedly, not the original Swedish – and if there is any form, shape, structure to the texts which leave our ateliers it's because I imposed it.'

Satamori indrew a hissing breath, and with it seemed to come all the chill of the northern winter (the Erikssons' home locked in Arctic night!) and the threat of Ragnarök that rode the flood-tide of the skelter. Some time passed.

Eventually Mustapha said, his tone thoughtful, 'One is inclined to wonder how the world views what one does . . For an artist, it's rare to be pleased that what he is proud of is anonymous and uncredited, but in this instance that paradox is the truth. It was painful to discover that all the tenets I had been brought up to were false. But I am not alone in that. What perhaps I may claim to be alone in, is that I did something about it.'

'I'm glad that you said nothing about this before,' Satamori snapped. 'I might not have – '

It sounded as though he was threatening to rise. Mustapha reached out a hand, unseen, to check him.

'My friend! Remember, I did not do what I did to insult you and your creed, only to give what light I could to the world after the light was stolen from my eyes.' A wave at his bright but sightless gaze, turned by sound to confront and transfix the older man.

'I . . . Yes, granted.' Satamori resumed his chair. 'Even so, I – '

'You still believe that doing honor to the ancestors is among a man's primary obligations. I will not contradict. I would prefer to – to *supplement*.' Mustapha's tone was persuasive without being downright wheedling, a narrow

37

path to walk with words. 'You must at least concede that it's better to honor the ancestors for what they did right than for the mistakes which, had they the chance, they would repent?'

Satamori hesitated. 'I believe I read a poem of yours on that subject,' he muttered. 'In translation, I'm afraid.'

Mustapha wanted to tremble – this was so close to what he had been worrying about within the past hour, the notion that someone would ultimately look at his work and see through it – but he overcame the impulse. Not a quaver showed in his voice as he answered, 'I am always glad when somebody reads and recalls my poetry, in whatever version. But do you not concede I have a valid point?'

'I suppose I have to.' Satamori heaved a deep sigh. 'I do believe it was the – the continuity of our beliefs which carried us through the terrible period after the Blowup; I do believe that if we hadn't had our respective faiths to use for crutches, we might never have risen again, even as far as we have done today.'

'On the other hand,' Mustapha said, 'it was because we held to the beliefs that we did, that we reached the point of striking out insanely in all directions, with some of our most terrible weapons. The Blowup is now two generations in the past, but it has left so deep a scar on the collective psyche of mankind that we will go to any lengths to avoid a repetition. For an intelligent young person today, it is more significant that we suffered a population crash corresponding with incredible precision to the example set by rabbits infected with myxomatosis, or lemmings, or indeed any species that has exceeded the ability of its environment to support it – think of coral and the crown-of-thorns starfish if you like! – it's more significant, as I was about to say, that we have thus been shown subject to natural laws than that idealistic dreamers in ancient times conceived of man as being superior to his animal cousins. Moreover, so many of us died. As we re-open the contaminated areas of the planet, we find we are walking through a giant graveyard. It is almost literally impossible to ignore the presence of our forebears' dead bodies.'

'You always had a sweet tongue, Mustapha,' Satamori said. 'Today you are excelling yourself; you've touched me on a very raw spot, too. Half of me knows, in my head, that one must fight the superstitious fear of death, or we shall forever be shut off from vast tracts of what are now again becoming habitable land – and we need that space, precisely because we did suffer a typical population crash. The other half of me stands in irrational awe of our ancestors, as though they had indeed become ghosts, or spirits, or whatever you call them, and ought not to be disturbed.'

He set aside his coffee-cup, now empty, and declined Ali's solicitous offer of a refill.

'On the other hand, by inventing the privateer Chaim did free us from that terrifying abolition of privacy which was so alarming to us we stopped at nothing to – But I said that to you before, and didn't convince you.'

'Nothing, I'm afraid, will convince me that applying the same principles which led to our near-suicide can rescue us from our remaining troubles,' Mustapha said in a tone of regret. 'I wish I could believe that. It would make life simpler, wouldn't it? But in fact I'm certain that only a complete re-assessment of our place on the planet, our relationship to other life-forms, in sum an abdication of our arrogance, will enable us to escape another, and another, and maybe another absolutely final, disaster similar to the Blowup. Skeptic though I am, I regard the teachings of the Way of Life as likely to encourage a proper humility in us, the sort of attitude that alone can permit us to survive.'

He gathered the skirts of his gown and rose.

'So I shall not attend Chaim's treasure-hunt party, even by direct invitation. I have no wish to see another generation of managers, bureaucrats and administrators wrap this species of ours in their steel-wire web of inflexible rules and regulations. I don't want to be party to the perpetuation of a system which condemned to death two-thirds of humanity. Better to expire of plague, starvation or cold than to be killed by the voluntary act of another man!'

'In so many ways I agree, and in so many I don't . . .' Satamori also rose, shaking his head; Mustapha could hear the faint brushing of his nape-hairs on the stiff collar of his formal coat.

'What it comes down to,' Mustapha said, 'is that mankind from now on must be governed by artists, not by politicians.

39

There is no other conceivable manner in which a survival-prone society can be organized. We must evolve an aesthetic of government, free from ideological trammels; we must commit our fate into the hands of those who derive artistic satisfaction from seeing a well-ordered community, who will crack their skulls into the small hours of the morning over a flaw in their scheme as I may worry myself sleepless over a line in a poem until it suddenly turns head over heels and comes out right.'

'You think those in power don't worry like that already?' Satamori countered wryly. 'Oh, we do – we do! But, since the subject of your work has arisen by implication, and I have an hour to waste before continuing to Chaim's, I should much enjoy another tour of your ateliers . . . ?'

'It will be my pleasure,' Mustapha said, bowing.

So they passed the next hour in walking around that part of Mustapha's home where his corps of assistants were at work. He had over a hundred now. They were orphans, of both sexes, whom he had recruited as little children – their parents being dead of violence or disease – and taught a trade that would furnish employment for a lifetime. Some worked in the scriptorium, copying out not only his poems but far more ancient texts, chiefly in Arabic though some in European languages for which they used a classic chancellery hand, and illuminated the result with tiny exquisite drawings based on models provided by the chief scribe, Muley Hassan. Others were busy in the paper-mill, converting old rags, straw, corn-husks and a score of miscellaneous vegetable substances into fresh new deckle-edged sheets. Still others worked in the bindery, where the air was pleasantly scented with glue and size, putting the final touches to the volumes which now commanded collector's prices the world around, irrespective of whether or not the buyer could read the contents.

Satamori fell instantly in love with a collection of old folk-tales and put down a deposit of five thousand to secure possession of it when it was finished and properly bound.

Once a fool who loved gold
  Killed his rival to possess
A lovely golden statue of a god.
  Afraid of being caught
  He melted the statue down
Saying fire could not destroy its worth.
  They found him starved to death
  In a waterless valley
His bare fingerbones clutching the gold.
  I do not call him foolish
  Because he could not eat gold
But because beauty is the food of the soul.

— MUSTAPHA SHARIF

Chapter 6

Hans was shaking as he entered his darkroom. It was always like this when he returned from one of his secret expeditions. He was on edge because he could never tell in advance whether he would have anything to show for the risk he had run.

It was getting harder and harder to purchase reliable film. The Economics Authority, of course, knew to the last centimeter how much was currently being manufactured, so for a project of this kind he had to depend on recuperated stock which all too often proved to have been fogged by radiation.

Neo-Polaroid was easier to come by; the available computing capacity was simply not up to determining whether or not a given buyer was telling the truth when he claimed he'd wasted half his last batch because he was drunk, and thrown the failed pictures in the garbage a month ago. But Hans would not have dared switch to it, because it had to be developed as soon as it was exposed. Carrying visual evidence of his surreptitious journeys would have been suicidal. A film could be blurred by springing the cap of its cassette – he had modified several specially, to make that

41

easier in an emergency – and he always took along decoy film too, exposed at places he was entitled to visit.

Dany, of course, was not party to his secret. She would have betrayed him in a fit of depression, without a doubt.

Humming, in total darkness but moving with the ease of long practice (and thinking about blindness while he worked, as he frequently did), he decided that for once he would process his important film first, not the decoy he had shot on his way to rendezvous with Mustapha. That could serve again. In any case he was suspicious of its quality. He prepared his developing bath, opened the cassette with a tingle of excitement –

And was suddenly dazzled by brilliant light as the door was flung wide.

He stood rigid as a rock, looking at the ruined film in his hand.

A shrill voice gnawed at his mind like a worm attacking the core of an apple.

'Hans, you were right about Athens! There's a public skelter terminal called Lyceum only they spell it a funny way. So I went there, but then somebody changed my card for another one and I can't figure this out either . . . Oh. Is something wrong?'

Gone: cobwebs. Gone: dust like snow unmarred by footprints. Gone: the irrecoverable 'after' to pair with the reconstructed 'before' . . .

In the next five seconds he came close to murdering his wife. But he changed his mind. He thought of something sweeter and more fitting. He tossed aside the film and turned, cordial of expression and tone.

'Well, what does the second card say?'

She proffered it uncertainly. Like the first, it bore a clue in rhyme. The answer, unless he was overlooking something ridiculously subtle, must be Oaxaca.

'Can you work it out?' Dany pressed. 'I do *so* much want to get to Aleuker's party!'

'Yes, I'm sure you do,' he agreed, moving forward as though to obtain a better light on the card. And continued, having drawn a deep breath: 'Only – what makes you think Aleuker will want you as a guest? He's inviting people intelligent enough to solve these puzzles for themselves: knowledgeable people, well-informed, interesting to be acquainted with. You, on the other hand, are stupid, silly, greedy, selfish, boring, and totally inconsiderate of other people. When you burst in on me just now, you wrecked something I set a lot of store by. It's gone past recall because you were too impatient to knock!'

'But I asked if anything was wrong!' In a wail. He ignored the interruption.

'So I think it would be a good idea if I kept out of your way for a while, because if I see you again today I shall certainly beat you to a whimpering pulp. I'll go to Aleuker's party. When I get back I may have sweated out my anger.'

'No! No, you wouldn't steal my chance!' Clawing at him with slow pudgy hands. He slapped her accurately on the left cheek, and as she shrank back, convinced by pain that he meant what he said, made for the skelter.

An echo of her curses seemed to follow him, though he knew that was impossible.

It was not a short trip, nor a quick one, but he relished the going.

At Oaxaca Concourse, overlooking the abandoned airport, it was raining, and there were cracks in the concrete roof of the skelter hall which allowed warm dirty water to drip down into many handle-less plastic buckets.

There a shabby young man exchanged the card Hans was carrying for still another, under the watchful eyes of the travel-hungry who pretended not to be: a vast group, hundreds strong, of so-called stucks, so terrified of skelter travel that they could not summon up the courage to pass the non-existent barrier dividing them from the clustered transit booths. It wasn't inability to pay that held them back; skelter travel cost nothing. Had to. There was no way of pricing infinite speed over nil net expenditure of power. And besides, mankind's resources of imagination and ingenuity had been slashed by far more than two-thirds when the population crash occurred, so it was imperative always to be able to bring the available talent to bear where it was needed.

The shabby man was contemptuous of the stucks, and let it show although he himself could no more use the skelters than could they. At least, however, his reason was tangible. He was a bracee, and the tell-tale glint of bright metal shone under the cuff of one loose sleeve. He was far from home, moreover; he had the flat face of a North Chinese, and when addressed returned a parroted phrase, recording-stiff: '*No hablo español!*'

He did not even know Hans had addressed him in English.

Wondering why he had been braced, guessing that it might have been for playing skelter roulette – he was the right age, had the right air of defiance, and, if he belonged to the culture one presumed had the right heritage of fatalism – Hans was reminded of Mustapha's protégés at Luxor.

For obvious reasons he seldom visited his co-conspirator's home, but he vividly recalled that first trip he had made in order to establish his credentials as a collector of books likely to increase in value. The excuse was colorable; he had had a part-share in an exceptionally good strike of technical equipment, mostly optical goods, in Southern Austria, and wanted a means of investing his windfall.

Granted that the children Mustapha took in and taught might otherwise have died in the gutter, granted that it must cost a vast amount every year to support them and purchase necessary supplies for the scriptorium and the bindery and the rest of the operation . . . Hans nonetheless had his own opinions about a setup which furnished so many nubile bed-companions. He was aware that Mustapha displayed the traditional Arabic indifference to their sex.

Still, he owed Mustapha the accomplishment of a burning ambition. No fee for that could be termed too high, regardless of what use the money was put to. And the link between those youngsters at Luxor and this barely-more-than-youth at Oaxaca was trivial: it summed to the suspicion that the person handing out Aleuker's cards might well be Mustapha's type.

Why had the notion occurred to him at all?

The reason was instantly obvious. He was wondering, half-unconsciously, what he would do if being deprived of her chance to attend Aleuker's party drove Dany to the pitch of leaving him.

44

Almost, he changed his mind and went home immediately. He was certain he would never again find himself a wife; there was far too much competition. (Curious, that an imbalance of five-to-three could create such liberty of choice for the minority!) But he steeled his resolution. It wasn't worth being married if he had to put up with the sort of thing Dany had just done to him. Better to live alone, rent a woman when he wanted to, maybe find a tolerable male companion to keep house – there was no shame attached to that, not nowadays...

In any case, he was being interrupted.

Some of the eyes which had fixed on him as he studied his new card did not belong to stucks. A loose group of about a dozen travelers, mostly youthful, had spotted him as he addressed the shabby man. No doubt they too were following Aleuker's trail. How many invitations could the man have issued? If the net had been cast wide enough to entangle Dany, logically thousands.

Therefore, too, there must be many eager-beavers who were pursuing imagined short-cuts, punching LNA codes into sub-legal computers for Aleuker's last notified address, or risking a bracelet by offering bribes to skelter-system officials who might have heard a rumor about the actual location of the party.

Among the group present was an attractive girl in her early twenties, a product of the fantastical mixing of the gene-pool the skelter had brought about. Her face alone hinted at ancestors from at least three continents. She whispered something to a male companion of her own age and advanced boldly toward Hans, swinging her hips against her long opaque dress and donning a flashing smile.

Ordinarily, like any other man of his generation, Hans would have preened a little and relished the chance to exchange a mere dozen words with her. Right now he was immune from feminine wiles. He strode directly back to the nearest vacant transit booth and punched a code as though he had solved the riddle at a glance.

In fact he had not; he had simply made for the Gozo public outlet, the code for which he had long ago memorized because Karl Bonetti received his patients in a former hotel

45

nearby, now rented out as offices. The skelter, inevitably, had killed the hotel business stone-dead. There was no need for anybody to rent a room overnight any more, no matter how far he might be from home. He could sleep in his own bed and work half a world away. Karl did precisely that. Hans had a vague idea that the psychiatrist actually lived somewhere in Greenland, but for good and sufficient reasons his home code was never divulged.

At the Gozo terminal Hans sat down on a stone bench and – with some enjoyment, which surprised him, because he had never before considered going to a treasure-hunt party – unraveled the complex double meanings of a mock haiku which led him to Pitcairn Island and another young man with more cards, even worse off than the one at Oaxaca. He was braced for the second time, and lacked his right hand as witness of the efficiency of the anti-tamper circuit in his first bracelet. Braced, one could enter a skelter . . . but that, or the attempt this young man presumably must have made to remove the metal ring, fired a shaped charge focused inwards.

Very messy.

At Pitcairn there were three recipients of cards hanging about, all too shy to approach Hans: one woman of early middle age, two men verging on the elderly, with that dusty air scholars seem to acquire regardless of their cultural back-ground through spending too much time in underpatronized libraries.

In any case, he would not have needed to re-use his dodge because he solved the new clue instantly: Bucarest. There was an excruciating pun on 'lei', obviously designed to misdirect the less perceptive into making for Honolulu. And from Bucarest he stepped into a private skelter in New Zealand, thinking that if Dany knew how close she'd been to her goal when she hit on Canterbury she would die of mortification. It would be great to tell her when he returned home, and watch her squirm –

He checked suddenly. He knew he had been given, now, a code for a private home, and it was in the right part of the world. He was walking on carpet in a spacious reception-hall nearly thirty meters long. Curtains were drawn across its windows even though hereabout there must still be a lot of daylight left; still, one knew that the planet's wealthy families no longer cared to be bothered by night and day.

But he was completely alone, and there was absolute dead silence, no matter how hard he strained his ears.

There were giants in the earth in those days.
The fact is attested by scriptural authority.
Today you or I can walk around the globe in three strides.
It does not follow that you and I have become giants.

            – MUSTAPHA SHARIF

Chapter 7

The declining sun dappled the sea with highlights as artificial-
looking as a Van Gogh painting. Reclining on a chaise-
longue, Chaim Aleuker admired it in between taking sips of
his planter's punch. He was the very model of elegant success:
lean, but nonetheless having contrived to develop a paunch;
extremely well dressed in a loose, casual shirt and breeches
of real silk, his hair immaculately coiffed, his fingers bright
with valuable antique rings.

His house – the largest of his three homes – overlooked
a small bay, or rather a cove, with a northwestern aspect.
On either side green-fledged hills ran down to stark gray
rocks, but there was a smooth sandy beach between. A sail-
boat and a power-launch bobbed at a tiny jetty. The scene
could have belonged to last century. There were few such
sights to be found now anywhere on Earth.

Around him, sitting or strolling or standing in knots of
two or three and chatting quietly, were the guests he had
invited to form a nucleus for his treasure-hunt party. It
was unlikely in the extreme that anybody new would arrive
before eight p.m. local – indeed, he had a bet with Boris
Pech of the Advancement Authority to that effect – and it
was not yet seven-thirty.

So, to keep him company, and also to assess the quality of any of the strangers who found their way through his careful maze of clues, he had notified some fifteen of his compeers to come direct. For a full generation after the Blowup personal power, influence and initiative had meant little; humanity existed in a totally-constrained situation where it was a real achievement to keep body and soul together . . . not that that phrase was current any longer. But now things were back on a more or less even keel. A new balance had been struck, new class-lines had been drawn, new meanings had been found for *rich* and *poor*.

In a very real sense, this handful of people, ten men and five women, could be said to be in charge of Earth. They had rescued most from the wreckage; they had laid down tracks on to which, with immense effort, society had been hoisted like a derailed locomotive. It was grunting forward again now, very cautiously in case there should prove to be other faults on the line . . . but making progress, after a fashion.

It was not a solution to everybody's taste, granted. The – the élite (much as Aleuker hated the word) numbered about one per cent of the surviving population. It was a simple fact, and stemmed from the terrible traumatic effect of the Blowup. Regardless of what reasons were offered by people to explain why they would have nothing to do with skelters, whether they invoked religious principles or a search for new roots or whatever else, the truth was definable in one word: fear.

Because they were afraid to share what actually was available to all, except those who had been given a bracelet for code-breaking, or using the system for theft or to cover up a murder, they sometimes became jealous and tried to sabotage the work of the new managers. Now and then a mob would attack a skelter outlet; now and then they would strike at rich individuals, preferring to level everybody down to their own mud-wallowing status rather than come up the free and open path to real achievement.

The élite was far too small. Its human resources were being stretched so hard one could hear them twang. Something had to be done to enlarge it. A casually amusing idea had cropped up recently in conversation: hold a treasure-hunt party, of the kind so much enjoyed by small-minded folk on the lowest rung of the skelter-using ladder, but instead of merely employing it as a trivial diversion, turn it into a genuine test for those with sharp minds and the desire to better themselves.

It was incontestably worth trying, though Aleuker himself had little hope of it paying off.

'Still expecting to win your bet with me, Chaim?' a voice demanded from his side.

The speaker was Boris Pech, affable, smart in blue suède, manager of the Advancement Authority which was the most recent of the planetary administrative departments. It had grown from a tiny nucleus within the Economics Authority, charged with devising new means of exploiting what the old world had left lying about in such colossal quantities: spare parts for obsolete machinery, adult toys for which there was no longer any call, gambling machines and the like. Boris Pech had hit on countless brand-new tricks, and elected himself automatically as head of the Advancement Authority when it was created five years ago.

Its work was little publicized; the climate of opinion was still against innovation. But sooner or later people would find out that it was still possible, in spite of all, to make progress.

Chaim chuckled. 'Only twenty minutes are left,' he said. 'And the clues we planted are pretty difficult . . . You were talking to Fred Satamori, weren't you? He was looking gloomy when he arrived; is something the matter with him?'

A waiter passed carrying a tray of drinks and canapés. Boris helped himself before replying.

'Not really, but in a way,' he said eventually.

'I see. You've caught the riddle-making habit, and now you're talking in mysterious gobbledegook.'

'On the contrary. I'm speaking the literal truth. Fred stopped off to see Mustapha Sharif on his way here, assuming he'd be among the guests and thinking they might come along together. You know he's been collecting Mustapha's work longer than almost anybody else.'

'Ah.' Chaim tapped the side of his glass thoughtfully with

one of his rings. 'Was Mustapha angry at not having been invited, is that it?'

'Not at all. Fred said he wouldn't have come even if he had been invited. He doesn't approve of our trying to perpetuate the – the managerial system we've evolved.'

'He finally came out and said it in so many words? That's interesting. And a little bit alarming.'

Boris blinked. 'I'm not with you!'

Chaim stretched, half-raising himself from the chaise-longue as though to cure an embryo attack of cramp. He said, 'Maybe I exaggerate, but I do believe Mustapha is a dangerous man. Has it never struck you that he's quite literally the only one of – of us, for want of a better term, who has succeeded in integrating himself into a non-skelter community?'

'That makes him dangerous? I'd have said the contrary! It's high time we –'

'Naturally, naturally!' Chaim interrupted. 'But how has he done it? By ingratiating himself; by what can only be called overt dishonesty. Have you ever attended one of those sessions he holds on the big Moslem feast days, when the imams come and recite the Koran all night long? He's not a believer. Hell, he edited most of what now passes for the authentic teaching of Prince Knud, and he doesn't believe in the Way of Life any more than you do! I take it you are still a good dialectical materialist?'

Boris chuckled. 'About as much as anybody, these days. I don't imagine Papa Lenin – let alone Grandpa Marx – would find much to agree with me about if we had a chance to chat together. But it did happen, didn't it, that the Soviet model came in handy when we had to try and reconstruct the world's economy?'

'Oh, we've stolen from it wholesale, under compulsion. If we hadn't forcibly redistributed the available resources, far more than two-thirds of mankind would have died; if we hadn't taken steps to interfere whenever some petty local power group decided to seek vengeance; if we hadn't made it worth the while of those with the necessary talent to work with us instead of against us, by creating the counterpart of a privileged group of Party members . . . No, we'd never

51

have made the repairs we have managed, makeshift though they are.'

'Mustapha won't concede the necessity, will he?'

'Indeed he won't. And I've never been quite sure why. I can't tell whether it's because he genuinely hates, on the gut level, everything about the old days and the old ways, or whether it's that he's secretly ambitious.'

Boris's mouth rounded into an O. He said after a pause, 'I recall a quotation, I think, though I can't remember the exact words. An English poet who said that people in his profession –'

'Ah, yes. "Unacknowledged lawgivers", isn't that it?'

'Yes, precisely. Was it Shelley?'

'I forget. But you're right to mention it in this context. At his home in Luxor, Mustapha behaves like a caliph, doesn't he? By acting out a role which the local people recognize, being unsophisticated enough to want a distinction between rich and poor, he has ingratiated himself, as I said. It is dishonest.'

Boris hesitated. He said, 'Even so, it's a white lie, surely. Life would be a lot easier for many of us, including yourself, if we did the same. It's no coincidence that so many of us now live on small islands, where one can get to know the local troublemakers personally and perhaps calm them down.'

'Bribe them to calm down?'

'Occasionally one has to. There's no alternative. It's as rigid a predicament as the world was in thirty years ago.'

'No, no and again no,' Chaim said. 'One thing we must *not* do is build the foundations of the future on deception. I know there are people who hate my guts just the other side of those hills.' He jerked a thumb over his shoulder. 'I can practically feel their breath on the nape of my neck sometimes: Maoris who ran for shelter in the cozy dead end of their old traditional ways, white people of British stock who were brought up to believe that their mother country was the greatest on earth and don't even yet accept that it doesn't exist any longer . . . Nominally I'm a Jew; that gives them enough reason to hate me, even though I bought my land legally, because they've always been convinced that any Jew with a fortune came by it dishonestly.

52

But the one thing we dare not be from now on is hypocritical, Boris! We musn't imitate the lies that brought the old world down, we mustn't pretend that riches are a burden, we mustn't deprecate intelligence, we mustn't preach loving brotherhood with a Bible in one hand and an H-bomb in the other!'

Boris gave a sober nod. 'We've taken steps in that direction. Making the skelter system free and open –'

'Hah!' Chaim gulped his drink. 'What does the village kid with ambitions see when he goes to a skelter outlet for the first time? Stucks, hundreds of them, and bracees, blocking his way! You know sometimes they attack people trying to get into a transit booth?'

'Yes, I've heard about that. We shall simply have to put guards on –'

'That's exactly what we must *not* do!' Chaim flared. 'Armed patrols at skelter terminals? I can't think of a worse way of importing the foulness of the past into what we hope and pray will be a brighter future! As a matter of fact, that was the chief reason why I agreed to organize this party. I'm desperately hoping that somebody may turn up who thinks in terms of no-guards, no-guns, no-locks. Come to that, no privateers. If we could only find a few people, just a handful, who've lived all their lives with the skelter as a fact, who've adjusted to it instead of regarding it as a fearful mechanical monster . . . ' Looking lugubrious, he shook his head.

'What you just said reminded me,' Boris murmured. 'How is your private venture in rehabilitation coming along?'

'What? Oh, the wild girl? Badly, damn it! In fact I'm minded to quit trying. I never realized before, not all the way down, how horrible the prejudices of the past must have been. Nor how crippling they could be to an innately intelligent child. I mean, she is effectively still a child. I've tried everything I can think of: persuasion, pleading, force of example, formal instruction, bribery . . . Doesn't work. They used to talk about people being afraid of their own shadow. What was done to her made her afraid of her own substance!'

'But she'll be around this evening?'

'I guess maybe. I told her to join us. Don't waste time on her, though. It won't be worth it.'

All of a sudden a melodious chime rang out from a bell mounted on the wall of the house, and everybody on the patio glanced reflexively in that direction. Instantly regaining his usual cordiality, Chaim jumped up, glancing at his watch.

'I just lost my bet! It isn't nearly eight o'clock yet, and somebody has found the way here! I wonder who it can be.'

INTERFACE H

Doubtless you know better O my beloved
Than to try and make me jealous of a rival.
The world holds so few intelligent lovely girls
I'd feel it selfish to keep one all to myself.
Do though choose for lovers men I can respect.
Otherwise I shall lose all respect for you.

— MUSTAPHA SHARIF

Chapter 8

At first puzzled, then becoming annoyed, Hans advanced
along the high-ceilinged room into which the skelter allegedly
belonging to Chaim Aleuker had delivered him. Its privateer
was off, which fitted with the notion of a party open to all
comers. The room, however, didn't. At the far end there
were long tables over which were draped lumpy white cloths,
concealing perhaps plates of food and glasses and bottles of
liquor; on the walls were fine pictures, of the sort one might
imagine Aleuker buying; but there was no sound, not even
music, nothing otherwise to suggest a festive celebration.

Was it just that by some miracle he had arrived ahead
of everybody else? Or was the whole affair a cruel hoax
after all? One had heard that in the rarefied atmosphere of
vast wealth and privilege people developed a distorted sense
of humor...

Then a door opened suddenly and a pair of servants
emerged: a footman and a maid in identical uniforms of
green trimmed with white braid. Both of them were braced,
of course; no one with free access to the skelter system had
reason to accept menial employment. The girl had a very
ugly face, and a scar ran down from her left temple to

55

vanish under the high collar of her jacket. Nonetheless her figure was excellent: full-bosomed, small-waisted, broad-hipped. Hans wondered briefly why she had been so stupid as to get braced when she could have had her pick of a thousand eager men.

They wished him a good evening – yes, of course, here it must indeed be early evening – and the footman requested a sight of the card which had brought him here. Having studied it, he asked Hans's name, repeated it under his breath, then beckoned the newcomer toward the windows that had been curtained until a second ago when the maid drew the drapes aside.

Revealed was a magnificent patio framed by greenery, with the sea beyond, where men and women in incredibly elegant clothing were gazing toward him with an air of expectancy.

Hans's mouth grew instantly dry. He had left home in such haste, he had not bothered to change out of his regular clothes: a short-sleeved shirt and crumpled pants of cotton drill, light enough to be tucked inside a climatized suit, the pockets of both bulging with uncounted oddments. More-over he was unshaven and his hair was in a bird's-nest tangle.

'This way, sir,' the footman urged. 'My employer is eager to make your acquaintance.'

It was too late to back down. Besides, he had already recognized the famous Aleuker, and he was indeed beaming with what seemed to be unfeigned pleasure. The maid slid aside a section of the floor-to-ceiling window, and in the footman's wake Hans passed through to confront his host.

Neither of them made any move to shake hands. The habit had been mislaid; there had been too many fatal contagious diseases. On the other hand, close friends kissed in public far more often than had been customary in the old Western culture: a gesture that converted mere liking into willingness to share risks. Very strange. Hans cursed his head for being crowded with irrelevant data. All these faces, some white, some brown, some yellow . . .

'A great pleasure!' Aleuker was saying warmly. 'I'm afraid I didn't quite catch your name when my man repeated it . . . ?'

'Hans Dykstra,' he heard himself mutter. 'I'm a re-cuperator, from – uh . . .'

He hesitated. Mentioning his profession was all right; it was respectable and respected, provided the practitioner was good at it. What he didn't know was whether it was correct form to refer to one's place of residence in a circle as exclusive as this one. Respect for privacy these days notoriously escalated in proportion to the square of one's wealth.

But Aleuker was looking expectant, so he completed the statement. 'From Malta. Valletta, to be exact.'

'Ah-hah? Haven't been there for ages,' Aleuker said, while Hans belatedly considered a corollary to his last assumption: suppose that obsession with the maintenance of privacy diminished as the means available to protect it increased? 'Used to have a boy-friend there. Maybe you know Christos Micallef?'

Hans shook his head.

'Lucky you. She's a thorough-going bitch.'

?

But before he could speak again a bell chimed, and Aleuker was suddenly looking past him, into the house, instead of at him.

'Hmm! Looks as though the rush is starting. I hope we didn't underestimate the numbers – we had the whole project computed, but . . . Well, that's my headache, not yours. Have a drink, make yourself at home, excuse me while I go welcome the number two.'

Small wonder, Hans realized as he turned and recognized the second arrival. It was the girl he had nearly met at Oaxaca. Aleuker was grinning from ear to ear. His jubilation faded a little, though, when her boy-friend followed her.

That should have been amusing. Hans, however, was in no mood to find anything funny. Frankly, he was scared at his own temerity. He was as out of place here as a diehard Christian at a Way of Life ritual. Maybe he ought to leave again at once?

No, the hell with that idea. He'd brazen it out for an hour at least, make himself scarce when his absence had lasted long enough for Dany to be contrite. His main pur-pose had been achieved: he was here, he'd spoken to Aleuker personally, even though he fully expected he'd be forgotten again in five minutes, and it wouldn't worry anybody if he hung around in some quiet corner for a while.

He advanced on a passing waiter and helped himself to a glass of wine, and, turning away, found himself being smiled at by a genial man in blue suède.

'Thanks for winning me my bet with Chaim!' he exclaimed. 'It's not every day of the year one can take money off that fellow. He insisted, you see, that according to his computers – mine really, but what the hell? – nobody would figure out those silly clues of his and arrive here before eight p.m. local. And then up you turn and blow his deadline to smithereens!'

'Uh – did I?' Hans muttered, restraining himself from consulting his watch because it would show some utterly irrelevant hour.

'Why, yes. You clocked in well under the wire,' the man in blue declared. 'By the way, I'm Boris Pech. Did I hear you say you're a recuperator?'

'Not *the* Boris Pech?' Hans blurted.

'What?' The older man blinked. 'Oh – oh, I guess you might say so. Advancement Authority, if that's what you mean. But I was about to ask you: do you ever work Europe, by any chance?'

'Uh . . . Yes, now and then. When we get clearance to dig over a zone that's been pronounced free of plague and radiation.'

'Ah. Then I wonder if you've come across anything that might help us out of a tight corner. We've combed North America, Russia, what little of Japan we can get at, without joy, and Europe's our last hope really, though I guess there may be something in Brazil . . . But of course Brazil is about the most unhealthy spot on the planet nowadays.'

'So I'm told,' Hans muttered. There was even less news from the interior of South America currently than from Central Africa or China. It was no simple case, like the latter two, of people having decided that skelters were evil and therefore being apt to slaughter skelter-travelers on sight; there were bloody wars in progress as a score of petty local lordlings tried to carve themselves new empires, massacring those who tried to resist.

'Well, the problem's this,' Pech went on. 'A bunch of us landed a skelter on the moon last year, as you know, and doubtless you've been wondering why so far we haven't made any use of the damn' thing!'

Hans nodded. He'd heard about that venture, announced as the first earnest of man's ability to surpass the scientific achievements of the pre-skelter period, which so many people still looked back to as a kind of Golden Age. But he had never expected to find himself chatting casually with one of the experts responsible.

Far off in his memory resonated something Dany had flung at him in a moment of inspiration during one of their frequent quarrels, and luckily never had the wit to re-use. It had wounded him. She'd charged that he was forever groveling at the feet of the past, scared of doing anything that might shape the future, even his personal future.

It was true he got little encouragement to act otherwise. His contact with people who had new ideas and the leverage to put them into effect was limited to reporting on the caches of industrial goods he unearthed. His task was to describe and identify them, not dictate what use they should be put to.

His one genuinely personal project would not be known until after his death . . . but that was merely sound sense, that decision.

Aloud he said, 'Yes, the point had been puzzling me. Why is it?'

'Because our best measurements haven't given us the transmission-span to closer than two centimeters plus or minus. Of course over such a long distance that's too slack by an order of magnitude. Earthside the problem doesn't exist; to be out by a couple of millimeters doesn't signify and one can compensate automatically for crustal tides and other minor nuisances. So what we've all been dreaming of is a batch of those ultra-high-precision lasers that Zeiss of Jena were alleged to be working on when . . . '

Hans let him rattle on. He had not had the vaguest notion that the moon's distance had been measured to within two centimeters, but he wasn't about to admit it. Nor, come to that, was he going to do a lot of talking during the party. He was going to compel himself to listen.

It was clear from the way Pech spoke that English was

no more his mother tongue than it was Hans's. Both he and Dany had been born to French and Flemish, he in Antwerp and she in a village near Liège.

But Pech used this language with a fluency and vocabulary which made Hans sound like a backward schoolboy, even though he had decreed to Dany when they first got married that they should use English in private as well as in public. She had agreed that the proposal was sensible. English was the first or second language of more people who had survived the Blowup than anything else bar Chinese and Swahili, neither of which had been scattered paint-spray-fashion around the globe. But it sat uncomfortably on his mind, and he remained terribly aware of how small an area of its immense richness he had learned to exploit. And if Pech was typical of Aleuker's friends . . .

He was. So Hans stuck by his resolution, and almost at once found it was both an advantage – for a patient listener was automatically defined as 'charming' – and a shame. He seldom got on easily with strangers, and he had fully expected Aleuker's friends to regard the treasure-hunt party as a joke. But they weren't in the least patronizing. They clearly assumed that anybody who solved the cryptic clues deserved to be treated as equally well-informed, equally intelligent.

That gave Hans a warm glow inside, marred only by the fact that he was obliged to stick to the 'good listener' rôle instead of – dare he? No! *No!* He must not mention what one day would add his own name to the roster of the famous, his secret project . . . (What the hell kind of wine was this, anyhow? Must be strong for him even to consider admitting the illegal things he was getting up to!)

Never mind. To be treated by the members of this in-group as an equal, however temporarily, was an accolade. News had begun to be acceptable again during the past decade or so, as the race's psychological sores began to heal, and with the dissolution of nations individuals made the headlines nowadays. Such individuals, in fact, as these: 'Fred, have you met Hans who was the first to find the party?' – and it was the Okinawan scientist Frederick Satamori, Deputy Director of the Skelter Authority (what would he think if he knew he was face to face with a criminal?); 'Ingrid dear, I hear you lost your cats! Does that mean there are none left now?' – and there he was commiserating with Dr Ingrid Castelnuovo the biologist who had just failed to rescue the domestic cat from extinction (and who was so much further along the Way of Life he was half-ashamed to admit his own adherence to the faith) . . .

He had imagined these persons to be unreal, because unapproachable, heard of but never in contact with anyone he himself might have met. Yet that notion had to have been false. This dozen-odd of Aleuker's closest friends, the winnowings of a vast acquaintanceship, these people with talents that would have been remarkable in any age, were mingling contentedly with the strangers who kept on pouring out of the unprivateered skelter – shy, plainly retiring men of advanced years who must have been through agonies of indecision before concluding that a chance to meet Chaim Aleuker made it worth taking advantage of the clues their scholarship enabled them to decipher; arrogant young student types clearly determined to prove they were a match for their elders; pretty un-bright girls, and a great many more pretty un-bright boys, who had ridden here on the shirt-tails of lovers with a higher IQ . . .

Fantastic. And a lot of fun. Hans's self-allotted hour was nearly up. He revised his deadline and decided to stay at least as long again.

INTERFACE I

Chapter 9

Cheerfully adrift on stimulating conversation, first-class liquor and delicious food – down here in the far south the sea still bred safe fish and much of the ground could be farmed in the old-fashioned manner provided it was protected from rain – Hans gloated privately over his vision of the morrow.

He was going to make Dany weep, actually weep, with his vivid description of the unique occasion she had cheated herself out of by ruining his precious film . . . not, of course, that she would have figured out the clues that led here. He would imply, in terms broad enough for her not to misconstrue, that he'd have been happy to escort her to the party, deftly link her into discussions beyond her range, help her to leave behind an impression that while that guy Dykstra's wife might not be too much to look at she must be pretty bright behind that quiet façade . . . He'd had to undertake similar chores for her throughout their married life, and since he was finding these élite strangers so pleasant he was confident he could have worked the trick in unprecedentedly distinguished company. For his benefit, if not hers.

He caught sight again of Frederick Satamori, on the far

side of the patio as he orbited from one primary of conversation to the next, always welcome, and thought of the enormity of the offenses he was committing by the scientist's standards.

This event would certainly have to be recorded in his secret files. One day somebody would read his account of this party and laugh aloud.

He had hoped for another chance to speak to Aleuker; he had an opening gambit ready, for the presence of many plants in tubs and pots on the broad patio hinted that the owner might follow the Way of Life. But the opportunity eluded him. Basking in adulation, the inventor seemed to be holding forth to a large group of admirers every time he passed within earshot of Hans: always a different group, but always the same subject – the privateer.

'When I think of what would have happened to the world without it . . . !' someone said loudly, and Hans cynically glossed: 'What about what happened to the world in spite of it?'

Not that he actually spoke the words. In fact he was overcome by a silent shudder of agreement. Stripped of virtually every other means of long-distance transport, because the industry did not exist to replace the aircraft and ocean-liners wiped out in the Blowup, let alone the tankers and freighters and cargo-planes, and there was not enough oil to run the remaining trucks and cars, and the railroads had been allowed to decay in most advanced countries, mankind had had no viable alternative to the skelter. It was cheap, not very difficult to build, and extremely reliable.

Yet it was itself the cause of the Blowup. Within a decade of being introduced it had turned sour. It had threatened to infect the human race with world-wide ochlophobia.

Early models had to be open to anybody who punched the proper code, whether friend or enemy, because it cost tens of thousands to activate the power-crystals. They were not designed to be switched on and off, only to resonate in a permanent state of excitement. If they were turned off, they had to be sent back to the factory to be energized again, and that would set you back three-quarters of your initial outlay.

In the terrible years following the Blowup it was touch and go whether any transportation system would survive, or whether every skelter on Earth would be smashed by crazy mobs sick of having bandits, criminals, JD's and even foreign soldiers pouring into their towns. It had been the West that hit on the idea of shipping saboteurs through the skelter into 'enemy' territory, but when the East retaliated the privileged few who owned domestic skelters at that time lived – if they did live – to regret their investment. Skelters in the Combloc were all public, and could be guarded.

Not that guarding them had made much difference in the long run...

In the tortured belief that an invention made in his own country of Sweden had brought about the downfall of civilization, Prince Knud had been driven to create the doctrines of the Way of Life, and scattered them by the millions of copies and in a hundred languages, at his own expense, to the far corners of the globe: a plea from the heart that humanity should cease chasing after gods and ideologies, learn to accept reality, recognize this near-Ragnarök as no more than the sort of population crash any species must endure if it over-bred.

Pleading failed. It took Aleuker's invention of the privateer to restore a semblance of sanity to the world.

Just in time, the skelter ceased to be a menace and became the means of reconstruction, tying together the isolated fragments of a shattered civilization. Now, code-trading was among the most heinous of 21st century offenses, enforced as much by public opinion as by the sketchy, disorganized laws still being cobbled together from the scraps of a dozen inconsistent legal traditions.

(At that house in Umeå: had it been spies or saboteurs who murdered the Erikssons? Mustapha had been convinced at once. On reflection, Hans found himself more ready to opt for criminals. Prisoners on the run before the advent of the bracelet would willingly have killed to make good their escape, and still more after its introduction, when the skelter was the only mode of getting away.)

But life was no longer intolerable. The resources which remained were being well exploited, and new ones were being discovered, and one's friends might as easily live on another continent as another street, which must be good. It would take a long time for mankind to digest its brutal lesson. At least, though, there was a culture which showed signs of evolving in a sane direction.

Hans gave a sage though slightly tipsy nod, telling himself solemnly that he was the guest of a universal benefactor and must not resent the fact that scores of other people kept getting between him and his host.

Tipsy? Hmm . . . Might be a good idea to go check out the food on display in the hall where he had first entered. There had been quiet music here on the patio for some time; within the past few minutes the volume had been turned up, and several couples were dancing. Moreover bright lights had been switched on, hidden among the trees or mounted on opposite, when it opened a few centimeters and light fell

He wandered indoors, possessed himself of a plate and allowed a servant to load it with smoked reindeer venison, fresh-cooked fish dressed with mayonnaise, and a crisp oriental salad, a typical contemporary combination. Hunger had smashed most of the barriers of prejudice that used to keep national cuisines apart. He ate with relish, wishing that at home he could afford to combine foodstuffs from three different parts of the world at every meal.

Having finished, and taken yet another glass of wine from a circulating tray, he leaned back in his chair. It looked as though it was about time for him to quit at long last. He was midway along the reception hall, between the skelter and the windows that stood ajar to the patio. For perhaps half an hour past no new arrivals had caused the soft bell to chime, and the privateer had been re-activated. It would make good sense not to stretch his luck.

Then, suddenly, all his resolutions dissolved in the blink of an eye.

He happened to be looking toward a door set in the wall opposite, when it opened a few centimeters and light fell on the face of a girl: large-eyed, shy as a fawn. She peered in, caught sight of him, and at once began to shut the door again.

Without conscious volition he found he had closed the

5   65

gap between them and was smiling at her from less than arm's length.

He heard his voice say, 'Hello!'

She answered in a language he hadn't heard for years – or rather, a dialect so close to it he understood perfectly. She muttered an excuse and tried to shut the door a second time.

He checked her by thrusting out his arm, and demanded fiercely, 'Are you Dutch? Or Flemish?'

Astonished, she let go the edge of the door and jerked her head back a trifle, those wide dark eyes fixed on his face.

'No – no, I'm from Brazil, but . . . '

Brazil?

It was too much for him to figure out. All he could concentrate on was her simple presence. She was short, slim, but well-shaped insofar as one could tell through the drab long dress she was wearing, a tremendous contrast to the gaudy finery of the other guests. Her face was oval, her mouth generous, her hair sleek and black, her hands delicate – in sum, she was beautiful. And young with it. She could have been any age from fourteen to twenty.

'Why are you hiding?' he rapped in his mother tongue. He reached for her hand, amazed at his own boldness. 'A girl as pretty as you should be the star of the party – come on!'

For a second she seemed inclined to resist. Then she yielded, and came out into the hall with the air of a wild animal, casting timid glances to every side. Hans was aware that he was the focus of attention: how did that man in the shabby work-clothes manage to conjure up *her*? He relished the sensation.

'You must have something to eat, and perhaps a glass of wine, and . . . ' Words he hadn't spoken for years came promptly to consciousness, and he was rewarded to hear her answer yes, yes please!

But it wasn't Dutch. It was the first cousin of Dutch, *Plattdütsh*. How in the world did she come to speak a dialect like that in Brazil?

From behind him, suddenly, Chaim Aleuker's voice: 'Hah! Hans, I see you found Barbara! Good luck to you, see if you can make her bloom a bit!'

Hans started so violently he nearly spilled the plate of

66

food he was loading for the girl, and swung around. But already Aleuker was past and vanishing in the direction of the patio.

'So you're called Barbara!' he exclaimed, having recovered his poise.

The girl shook her head vigorously. 'No, my name is Anneliese Schenker.'

'But I'm sure Chaim called you –'

'It is a joke for him. He says that "Barbara" means "a wild girl" – and he thinks I'm a savage!'

There was a red ring of anger in her voice; she set her shoulders back and folded her fists and glared after Aleuker.

Hans hesitated only a moment. Then he said, 'I suspect you may want to tell somebody about yourself. And it cannot be easy to find people who speak your language. I do, more or less. Shall we go and sit over there out of the way? I promise I will listen to whatever you say.'

He handed her the plate of food. She took it, her eyes on his face, and after a miniature eternity said, 'Yes, please, sir. I would be so glad if I could talk to somebody properly instead of struggling with English that I only half understand.'

Incredible, incredible! I'm holding a *tête-à-tête* conversation with this girl every susceptible male in the place is eyeing . . . How did it happen? Never mind! Enjoy, enjoy!

He concentrated on the tale she was unfolding.

She did indeed come from Brazil. The reason she spoke a language so close to his was that she was descended from a colony of German protestant fundamentalists who after World War I had decided they must cut themselves off from the fleshpots of wicked Europe and live a holy life in a new land.

Hans's mind boggled at the realization that he was talking to a Christian. This was like being transported back in time!

Refusing to accept cars, radios, telephones – let alone the skelter – with hand-axes and horse-ploughs they had built a flourishing little town a hundred miles from anywhere, and called it Festeburg: after a religious song, she explained.

They traded produce locally, and once or twice a year

they loaded a boat with vegetables, cloth and handicrafts, and rowed it down-river to a market-town where they bartered for tools, nails, wire and other goods, mostly metal, which they could not manufacture themselves. Aside from that they had no contact with the larger world.

She had been told by her grandfather how news of the 1939 war reached the colony, by word of mouth and the accident of a newspaper wrapped around a packet of seeds, and how the *Predikant* called everyone together for a day and a night and a day of non-stop prayer to avert God's wrath from his most faithful worshippers.

The trick must have worked; at any rate the second world war passed and nothing changed in Festeburg.

Prayer was less successful in the case of an epidemic which struck the community and killed Anneliese's mother when she was still a child. From her halting descriptions Hans deduced that the disease might have been influenza-M, third of the four deadly new strains hatched in the uplands of New Guinea which spread like wildfire after the introduction of the skelter, or just possibly a late outbreak of Alaskan croup. He didn't inquire over-closely, though. He was too busy marveling at the chance which had brought him an emissary from the past he had imagined vanished forever. Until only a couple of months ago this girl had lived in the pre-skelter age! In cultural terms she had been further removed from the modern world than the Erikssons, whose bodies he had disposed of earlier today. (Yesterday? What the hell?)

'What happened to bring you here?' he urged.

Bit by reluctant bit, she explained. Somewhere in the *sertão* a minor warlord had begun to carve out an empire in the all-too-typical manner. Among the places he coveted was the site of Festeburg.

There had been a siege. Her father had been killed. Her elder brother, then head of the family, ordered her to take a canoe and paddle down-river in search of help. With unbelievable courage, considering she had never been further from home than she could walk in half a day, she obeyed.

The first people she had come on were friends of Chaim Aleuker's cocking a snook at the dangers of modern South America by taking a camping vacation . . . but with the aid of a portable skelter. (Hans pursed his lips at that. A traveling skelter had to incorporate its own range-finding gear, and cost a million if you could find a technician able to build one for you.)

They hauled her out of the river when her canoe sprang a leak after hitting a submerged snag, but they couldn't talk to her until Aleuker turned up. She said she thought it was a miracle when he stepped from the coffin-sized box in the middle of the camp-site. She had literally never dreamed of a skelter before.

But she thought it was even more miraculous when it turned out Aleuker spoke Yiddish and was able to communicate with her in a rudimentary fashion. She had been aware that other languages existed apart from the German dialect spoken at Festeburg, for the traders they dealt with spoke corrupt Portuguese, but girls were forbidden to talk to strangers.

Having puzzled out her story, Chaim persuaded his companions to collect their guns and set off for Festeburg. When they arrived there, however, they found it burning, its inhabitants exterminated.

Well . . . too bad! Everyone in the group had business to attend to, and their vacation was too near its close for them to bother about the departed warlord and his troops. So in sheer despair, shaking with terror, she had let Chaim lead her into the skelter and bring her here.

In other words: to a place which, according to everything she had been brought up to believe, was a fair facsimile of hell.

I am ashamed that I want to believe in judgment.
Punishment turns my guts sour and I will not condemn.
If I did I would be among the guiltiest of all.
I am not however ashamed that those I would like to punish
Are those whose crime is despoiling their fellow men
And particularly little children of the rightful joy
They should have from the existence of their bodies.

              – MUSTAPHA SHARIF

Chapter 10

Perhaps it was unfair to Aleuker – perhaps Hans was adding unjustified glosses to what the girl told him, and in fact she was seeing rapists around every corner, as a result of her appalling heritage . . . but the impression was quite clear that when Aleuker discovered that Anneliese wasn't minded to pile straight into bed and make wild jungle love he lost interest.

One would assume that Aleuker had a normal healthy appetite for women; indeed, one had heard that because of his fame he'd enjoyed far more of them than his proper share, which statistically must be three-fifths of one, sixty per cent, or thirty per cent of each of two, or fifteen per cent of each of four . . . The deadpan calculation made Hans want to giggle.

Serious for a moment, he wondered what it would be like to be in Aleuker's shoes, welcomed as a father for the babies of women around the world. Those lucky potential mothers who had proved to be naturally immune to CPF – which Dany was not, and in consequence had been compulsorily sterilized – picked and chose their mates regardless of marriage, regardless of stern official warnings about letting so much of the gene-pool go to waste.

Once, three years ago, without informing Dany, he had advertised himself in one of the crudely-printed contact journals that circulated from continent to continent, serving another and more valid purpose beside the ostensible one of linking people with unusual sexual tastes. With so few people left it seemed a shame that he, Hans Dykstra, should leave behind no child at all, whether or not he could bring it up personally.

But the only girl who had answered had failed to show at the rendezvous he'd proposed in Canberra, and he'd felt so silly he'd never repeated the experiment.

Plainly it would be just as stupid to mention that to Anneliese as it would have been to tell Dany. He composed himself to go on listening.

She had clung to Aleuker purely because she didn't know where else to go. Like most Christians she had been taught to believe that even followers of heretic branches of her own faith were children of the Evil One and eternally damned, so finding herself in a world full of what she termed heathens, who drank liquor, and smoked, and fornicated, and bowed down to false gods, specifically to trees and animals, had come close to driving her out of her mind.

Only the fact that she hadn't spoken to anybody for weeks – bar a few sour exchanges with Aleuker and his servants – had impelled her to join the party, as she'd been told to. All the time she was talking her eyes kept darting from the sight of one abomination to another, and her cheeks remained as pale as paper.

When he had the chance, Hans demanded how old she was. She muttered, 'Seventeen. Eighteen soon.'

At that age, to have seen her father killed, her home burned, all her friends slaughtered . . . ! That echoed an ancient nightmare of Hans's. He himself had been orphaned in the last epidemic of CPF, and watched his mother die screaming. Though he had found kindly foster-parents instead of being dumped in one of the children's camps that were the breeding grounds for 21st century crime, his loss

retained the power to wake him weeping in the night now he
he was well past thirty.

Dany had never sympathized with him, only complained
at having her own sleep disturbed.

But he suspected that this girl might understand instead of
mocking a grown man for shedding tears . . .

Suddenly, with no warning, there was a bang. The conversation flowing merrily in and outside the hall snapped off
short like a dry stick trodden on by a heavy foot.

Somebody said into the near-silence which followed, 'Hell,
that was a gun!'

There was a concerted rush toward the sliding windows
giving access to the patio – and instantly a mêlée, as those
wanting to go out met those wanting desperately to come in.

There was a confused sound of shouting; the guests pushed
and milled, and Anneliese laid her hand on Hans's, whisper-
ing, 'Is something wrong?'

He relished the touch of her fingers: so light, so warm,
so delicate. It was as though he could literally feel the
fragrance of her fresh youthful body. The impact on him
was like a drug.

Rising, daring to lay his own hand on her soft hair in
a gesture midway between a pat of reassurance and an overt
caress, he said, 'I'll ask somebody. Don't worry – '

But too late. Another bang cleft the air, and a whole
more-than-man-high pane of the sliding windows shattered.
Hans had an instantaneous vision of half a hundred mouths
standing ajar in astonishment –

And then everybody between him and the outside dived
flat to the floor, affording a clear sight of what lay beyond.

At the mouth of the little cove overlooked by Aleuker's
house, a pair of small headlands bent to the sea, dark on
dark but highlighted by the beams of a newly risen moon.

Between them, as though targeted in the sight of a rifle,
three clusters of bright red-yellow flame admired their own
reflections in the water.

The music had stopped. One could hear yells of savage
anger. The wavering flames fell into place in Hans's mind.

War-canoes!

72

He'd been vaguely aware for years that among the Maoris – as among virtually every ethnic group which had contrived to preserve a precarious identity distinct from the otherwise all-pervading culture of the Christian West – there was a violent new cult dedicated to vengeance. There were few unassimilated Maoris, however, even after their ranks had been swelled by half-caste defectors from the white-biased culture of New Zealand, and he had never expected that they would be the people to launch an attack and trap *him* in it.

But then he had only been to New Zealand twice before.

A long time seemed to pass, though it could have been at most a few heartbeats, during which he felt his jaw hang foolishly loose, his gape matching that of everybody else in view. The spasm of paralysis was ended by not one but this time a barrage of shots, and a scream that peaked into the treble though it began in the baritone, the voice of a man in mortal agony.

The war-canoes had reached the shore and the torches were heading for the house. Rhythmical chanting rang out, paced by the stamping of many feet. As though terror had endowed him with telescopic vision, Hans saw a score of nearly-naked brown men, some clutching guns, others spears, with necklaces of human teeth around their necks.

At the top of his voice Aleuker shouted, 'Keep calm! I have machinegun posts –'

And the words were cut short by the sewing-machine vibration of those machineguns, stitching lines of death across the ranks of the attacking force.

Nonetheless, they had already achieved part of their goal. Three of the guests were coughing away their life-blood on Aleuker's beautiful patio; others were sobbing and moaning from minor injuries; and now the torches – soaked in oil, no doubt – were being put to their proper purpose: they arced through the air and came landing on the roof of the house, thud-thud-thud.

'Sir, please, what is happening?' Anneliese whimpered, clutching at Hans.

He recovered his presence of mind with an effort, glanced down at her, and in the same moment saw that the skelter was a mere five steps away. It wouldn't be more than a few seconds before someone else thought of making a run for it.

'Come on!' he blasted, dragging the girl to her feet, and pushed her furiously toward their way of escape.

'But I don't want to –'

'Stay and you'll get killed!' Hans retorted, and forced her into the booth, his fingers automatically seeking the code for his home at Valletta. No time to think of what Dany would say; all that mattered was to flee.

Howls, shots, the crackle of flames taking hold, all vanished instantly –

And Anneliese screamed.

Hans wanted to, as well.

They were in his hallway. Facing the skelter, in the same chair where she had awaited his return from Sweden, as though she had arranged herself with care so this must be absolutely the first thing his eyes lit on: Dany.

Or rather, Dany's body.

She had cut her wrists and was saturated waist to feet with drying blood.

Incomprehensibly
Our ancestors preferred
Putrefaction over evolution.
They were embalmed
Wrapped in sheets of lead
Or stored in coffins in a vault.
When my time comes
I want to grow into a stalk,
A leaf, a flower and an ear of corn.

— MUSTAPHA SHARIF

Chapter 11

His reaction was pure reflex, without calculation. His left hand flew up to cover Anneliese's eyes while his right stabbed another code into the skelter, and between one breath and the next they were bitterly cold.

'Error! Transmission error! Sometimes happens – nothing is perfect, I think I must have drunk too much, terribly sorry, what a horrible sight to have run across by accident!' Gabbling. He heard her moan a little, but she was too overcome to form words.

At least, though, here in Sweden it was briefly light, low sun glinting on the snow-ridges beyond the windows. And the Erikssons' corpses had safely gone to be incinerated. He could take her by the hand and lead her passive into the living-zone, inventing frantic reasons for the state of the house.

Her teeth chattered although the weak sunlight had raised the temperature above the freezing point. He continued with his meant-to-be-soothing flow of talk.

'Get fire going in a second, don't worry, I'll take care of everything . . .'

On the stone hearth, logs half-charred, ancient ash. He

thought of the correspondence paper in the study, ran for it leaving her to stare wide-eyed and amazed at the dust, collected the entire stack and came back carrying a sort of torch already lighted at the end with the betraying truth about the ownership of the house. Damp, it burned poorly. But it did burn. (Goodbye the sheet to be featured in my secret files . . .) In a box beside the fireplace, kindling which had rotted but not crumbled.

His hands trembled. He hadn't built a fire in twenty years.

'I'll turn on the main heating in a moment,' he promised. 'I don't come here often, you see. People don't stay in one spot these days – I imagine Aleuker told you – we like to follow the warmer weather because it's so easy and quick to travel, so in winter of course you leave places like this empty until the spring, head for a warmer climate . . . '

She was shaking, *shaking*. Near the fireplace there was a low stool; she groped her way to it and sat down. The kindling caught and flames leapt high and yellow. (In imagination he could hear screams. Had the Maori extremists trapped many of his fellow guests in the pyre of Aleuker's home? He shut off that line of thought.)

There were other questions bombarding him, such as how to conceal the lack of electricity. With relief he realized: she isn't used to power, but I ought not to have mentioned the main heating for fear the oil is circulated by an electric pump!

'Are there still policemen in your world?' she said suddenly.

What? Hunkered down, tending the fire, he swiveled to face her.

'You should tell the police about that dead woman,' she went on.

'How can I?' The lie was instantly tailored. 'I told you, we were taken there by a transmission error. Probably my fault as I said for having drunk too much, but even so . . . No, I might try a million skelter codes and never find my way back to the same place. I don't even know what country we were in.'

Numbed by the cold, his fingers ached. He spread them at the fireside to rescue sensation. The chill referred to ghastly experiences in his childhood. Was it really so short a time ago, could the world really have improved so much since he was a ragged and half-starved waif?

'You don't even know what country?' she repeated dully after a pause.

'No, of course not. The skelter can take you anywhere in next to no time.'

She pondered that for a while, eventually gave a nod and went on staring at the flames.

'Sorry about the mess everywhere,' he ventured. 'Like I said, I don't come here very often.'

'Then why did you bring us here now?'

'Uh . . . ' Yes, why? Quickly, quickly, a convincing reason despite the fog of alcohol. 'Well, obviously we had to get away from Aleuker's place, didn't we? And what's more' – gravely, with an air of considerateness, fine! – 'you haven't had much chance to adapt to our modern world, according to what you told me. You've been overwhelmed by new ideas and new habits ever since Aleuker took you to New Zealand –'

'*New Zealand?*' A cry. She jolted around on her stool.

'Why . . . yes! Did you not even know where you were?'

Dumbly she shook her head. And forced out at length, 'I thought maybe . . . the United States?'

The horizons of another world, Hans thought. With the concept came a sense of fresh confidence. The image of Dany's corpse, so brilliantly red in his imagination, was a warning that the universe was poised to come crashing on his head. There was no real sense of loss involved; he had never actually loved his wife, just wanted to have *a wife* in an age when so many men were resigned to never achieving that goal.

But if no one apart from this ignorant girl so far knew that he had seen Dany dead, it shouldn't be too hard to wriggle out from under the consequences.

The first step must be to mislead her away from understanding what she had seen. He drew a deep breath and rose to his feet.

Excusing himself, he went to inspect the heating system.

By a minor miracle, it was self-feeding, with a compressed air tank to start the process that required only a dozen firm strokes of a plunger, like an overgrown camping stove. A yellowish smoky flame answered the application of his lighter, turning blue as the burner scorched itself free of dust, and when he returned to the living-zone the registers were already uttering the first warm air.

Pausing in the doorway, he looked around with a grimace.

'I should apologize! I'd no idea the place would get so filthy in such a short time . . . It must be very different here, by the way, than where you hail from.'

'Where is here?' she asked tremulously.

A brief hesitation. Safe? Well, worth risking, to gain her confidence.

'We've come to Sweden.'

Her response was a distracted nod. The gamble had paid off. For her, no doubt, it was a name on an old map, corners ragged from the attentions of termites, lacking referents.

She said, 'No, not very different. Also at Festeburg nothing could be left for more than a day or two without becoming very dirty . . . Is that snow?'

She was gazing at the windows.

'Snow? Yes, of course it is!'

'I heard about it. But I never saw any before.'

Hans relaxed so violently he almost gasped. It was going to be easier than he'd dared to dream, convincing this youngster he was telling the truth about Dany. His mind fermented with ideas: leave her here, afraid to use the skelter without a companion, trapped for as long as proved necessary to sort things out . . . There was no evidence of his illegal trips, even in his dark-room, for the police to find; he could ask Karl Bonetti to confirm that Dany had made scores of suicide threats without putting any of them into practice; he could arrange to have his hallway redecorated so Anneliese wouldn't recognize anything, or better yet he could move to another country, another continent . . .

It could all be done in forty-eight hours.

Too bad that he would have to sacrifice the would-have-been star entry in his secret files – but at the very edge of his mind hovered the idea that from now on he might not be paying so much attention to his hobby.

This girl Anneliese: given the way she'd been brought up, she might well be susceptible to the ancient notion that marriage was a woman's only security. What would she desire more than security in this weird, unfamiliar world?

To have a young bride . . . Ho, *ho!* It must be a decade or more since a man in his thirties married a girl of seventeen!

He took a frenzied grip on himself, aware that he was still a little drunk despite the sobering shock of seeing Aleuker's home attacked, and then finding Dany. It was too soon to let his dreams run away with him.

He said, 'Anneliese – dear – I think you look tired. Should I prepare a bed for you? There's a room you can sleep in, over there.'

He pointed toward the child's room, forgetting that he'd left its door ajar and the weak sunlight would reveal the toys, books and scattered clothes. She smiled and turned her head, and instantly was bewildered.

'You – you are married? You have children?'

Invention, quickly! Something that can't be used against me!

His tone was so smooth it astonished him as he replied.

'Ah, this is my old family home. You heard that there was – well, what we call the Blowup? And after that, plagues and epidemics?'

A nod. 'I don't understand much about it, but they did tell me. It must have been very terrible.'

'Yes, it was. . . . Well, I had a sister. She died. And my parents are dead as well. I – ah – I never felt inclined to change things here, if you see what I mean.'

'Yes, I think so.'

'But it was a long time ago. It's foolish to live with the dead past. Now you are here, I have an excuse to clear away what I kept as mementos – no, sit down! Stay by the fire!' Pushing her gently, one hand on her soft warm shoulder. Somehow his fingers remained in contact with her and they were looking at each other, eyes direct into eyes.

There was a stillness.

'Poor little girl,' Hans said at last. 'To be cast adrift in this strange world . . . it must be awful. Trust me, though, and I'll see you come to no harm.'

Unexpectedly from her bright dark eyes a pair of tears spilled over.

'Thank you, sir,' she muttered almost inaudibly.

79

'Not sir! Call me Hans!'

'Yes please. If you don't mind . . . ? Yes, it is a fearful new world for me, and I know so little about it. I can't even find my way around, let alone make a living for myself. It is very kind of you to show such charity. You will be blessed.'

Upon which, with a sudden withdrawal into herself, she freed her arm from his touch and returned to her stool, gazing once more into the fire.

So many things that might contradict his lies! Letters with Eriksson's name and address on – the rotting food from the deep-freeze, clearly stamped for consumption at the latest by forty years ago – irreplaceable newspapers which must go because though ignorant of Swedish Anneliese might read the dates on them, too . . .

It hurt him, it agonized him, to see these precious relics destroyed. But he drove himself to the task, mindful of Dany's corpse waiting for him at home.

And other things had to go as well, for fear she might think to ask him later why, if he had been born in Belgium, his 'family home' should be in Sweden. The little girl's books, punctiliously signed – her name had been Greta – though not her clothes, or not all of them, for she had been tall and well-built for her age while Anneliese was slight for hers, so some of them might come in useful. Doubtless at Festeburg with its limited resources, long before the same thing happened in the larger world, one had had to be content with other people's cast-offs . . .

He breathed a vast sigh of relief on discovering that the girl had abandoned her stool for a long sofa, and lying on it had dozed off. That made his job far easier.

The deceased master of the house had owned a large wardrobe. He had been taller than Hans and rather fatter, but providentially took the same size in shoes. Warm in musty thick winter garments, Hans was able to trudge outside with those few articles he did not want to leave lying around for Anneliese to inquire about, yet dared not send to the incinerators for fear they would survive the flames and be recognized as antique. Most of these were luxury items, chiefly molded cosmetic jars and perfume bottles.

80

He could have smashed them, but the noise might have awakened Anneliese.

The ground was frozen far too hard for him to dig a hole; for the time being he'd have to be content with hiding them in the snow.

Returning, bitterly cold, he found bedding and made up the child's bed for her; she was short enough to find it tolerable, he judged. Then he carried her from the living-zone and tucked her in, removing only her shoes. She barely stirred, being deeply asleep by now.

His mind was full to the brim with two competing emotions: a sort of frustrated tenderness, as though this were his own child he was putting to bed, and a cold and calculating plan for the future, a tangled skein of deceit climaxing in arson to explain why eventually they would be unable to come back here . . .

At the edge of hearing: trickle, splash . . . What in the world? Oh, of course. A pipe frost-fractured in the main bathroom. The toilet pan, he found, had been frozen, predictably enough; now a wedge of ice bobbed in it as water dribbled down from the flushing valve behind.

But the Erikssons had been careful people. It took only minutes to locate a tool-kit in a kitchen drawer, which included a roll of siliconized tape. After making the repair, crudely but effectively, he inspected all the other piping he could find and concluded that there was no risk of further leaks.

Now, before leaving: what else? Obviously, light for Anneliese if she woke while he was gone and the short sub-arctic day was over. Festeburg had never accepted electricity, so she would be used to candles, and here were several, wicks damp and fizzing, all colors of the rainbow, meant for *tête-à-tête* dinner parties, not real illumination – but never mind. He set one by the bed, and matches which (he tried one) still struck well after all these years.

That, and a quick note telling her not to worry, he'd be back soon, would have to be that. He dared not delay too long before reporting Dany's death, even though the Maori attack on Aleuker's home would make it extremely improbable that anybody had noted the exact time of his departure from New Zealand. He had a good cover story, too; he would say that even if he fled he realized he didn't want to confront Dany after their disagreement, so he made for the Gozo outlet instead and spent a while debating with himself as to whether he should ask Karl Bonetti to examine her and pronounce on her sanity. Then decided against the idea, and finally made for home, to discover ...

Yes, the claim would carry conviction, but only if he hurried now.

He propped up his note beside the candle, and on impulse kissed Anneliese's forehead. She half-smiled in her sleep. As he turned away his heart ached with yearning and delight.

It was laid down
That making the *hajj* to Mecca
Earned much merit for a man
Someone I know
Now makes the *hajj* twice a day
It takes about one minute thirty seconds

— MUSTAPHA SHARIF

Chapter 12

He walked straight past the disgusting ruin of Dany, heading for the phone. He dialed the police emergency code, and waited. Sometimes the phones in Valletta worked, and sometimes they didn't.

This time they worked. A voice said grumpily, 'Yes, police.'

'Please send somebody here right away,' Hans said, his voice shaking just a little. 'It's my wife. She's dead.'

'What?'

'She must have killed herself while I was out. Here, make a note of my skelter code. I'll disconnect the privateer.'

Less than two minutes later a uniformed sergeant appeared in the skelter, holding up a portable recorder. He said, 'Repeat after me, please: I Hans Dykstra – do of my own free will – consent to the use of my skelter code – by law-enforcement officers – and understand – that on completion of these inquiries – I may require another code – confidential from the authorities ... Thank you.'

He stepped into the hallway, his eyes fixed in dismay on Dany. A moment later another policeman appeared, and then after a slightly longer delay a harassed-looking man carrying a medical kit, immediately followed by a photographer.

The second policeman to arrive identified himself as Chief Inspector Vanzetti; he was a portly man with tired eyes, his summerweight uniform patched with sweat although it was locally winter.

'Tell me exactly what happened,' he invited.

Hans licked his lips. 'I – uh – I guess I found her about two or three minutes before I was able to call up. I had to go in the bathroom and vomit. The shock, you understand. And . . . Well, I wasn't feeling too good in any case. You may have heard Chaim Aleuker held a treasure-hunt party?'

Vanzetti's eyes widened. 'You were at it? Hmm! How come you got away with a whole skin?'

'Did it turn out to be bad?'

'Twelve deaths that we've heard about, most of his house destroyed . . . How *did* you get away?'

Hans felt his cheeks start to burn. He wasn't sorry. A little visible embarrassment would support his story well.

'I hate to admit it, but . . . Well, you see, I'd been there three hours, maybe four, and I'd drunk a lot, and – and when the shooting started I just plain ran like hell. I'm not sure, but I think I was probably the first person to think of making for the skelter.'

'That's interesting,' Vanzetti muttered. He consulted the watch on his wrist: no ordinary watch, as Hans's expert eyes informed him, but a classic Seiko Worldtime, the like of which had not been built since the Blowup. 'That means you must have left New Zealand at least an hour and a half ago, doesn't it?'

'I didn't come straight here.'

'Why not? And where did you go?'

'I didn't come here because Dany and I had had a row. I'm a photographer in my spare time. She was going to this treasure-hunt party – she didn't tell me who the host was, and I'd assumed it was one of her abominable friends and preferred to stay at home and develop some film I was specially proud of. She barged into my darkroom and ruined the film, and I decided . . . ' He hesitated. 'I decided I'd take the clue-card and go to the party myself, to even things up.

Now I'm terribly ashamed of myself. But I swear I never dreamed she might do this!'

He gestured at the corpse, around which the doctor and the photographer were prowling like carrion-crows, poised to dart in and dash back again.

'You had no idea at all?' Vanzetti probed.

'She had threatened to kill herself,' Hans muttered. 'But never tried it. I consulted Karl Bonetti about her, and he said – Oh, that's where I went. That's why I didn't come straight home. My wife's mental condition had been on my mind during the party, and like I say I was rather drunk when I left, and – well, for no real conscious reason it struck me as a good idea to go to Gozo. I know the code for the public outlet there nearly as well as I know my own; Dr Bonetti is an old friend of mine.'

'Did you actually see him?'

'No, I wandered around brooding for a while and eventually decided it was worth making one more try to patch up the row. So I came home and – and I found her.'

'Chief,' the sergeant said, 'it's suicide. Not a shred of doubt. She used this.' He held up a bright oblong partly smeared with dry blood. 'An old-fashioned double-edged razor-blade. She cut her thumb and finger with it while she was slashing her wrists.'

Vanzetti nodded. 'Doc, do you agree?'

The doctor grunted what might have been an affirmative, and went on studying the corpse with instruments from his kit.

'How long since she died, would you say?' Vanzetti probed.

'Oh . . . Not less than three hours, not more than five. I'm just checking to see what she took beforehand: a stimulant pill or two, I imagine, and possibly some liquor too . . . Ah, here we are.' He straightened, holding up a little glass tube with a trace of blood on the lower end, containing a thread of some whitish chemical mixture that had turned color at two levels, blue and green respectively.

'Yes, she was both drunk and doped. A mix that could have done awful things to her head.'

'You said,' Vanzetti went on, turning to Hans again, 'you'd consulted Dr Bonetti about your wife?'

'Ah . . . Yes, more than once. He said her suicide threats were so much noise, an attempt to make me pay more attention to her.' Hans hesitated. 'It's – uh – it's not much of a secret among our friends that there'd been friction between us this past year. I'd better make a clean breast of that. You're bound to be told sooner or later.'

'Oh, I don't believe our inquiries need be very extensive, given what you just heard. Naturally there must be an inquest, but there's no call to worry overmuch about that. It'll be largely a formal matter.' Vanzetti shook his head dolefully. 'A terrible thing, this. Terrible! Now, about Aleuker's party: who can confirm you were there at the relevant time?'

'Well, Aleuker himself – '

'No, I'm afraid not. He's dead.'

'*What?*'

'He was shot. The first of the dead to be identified. The news had just come in by satellite when I left headquarters. A terrible loss for us all!'

Hans folded his hands into fists and stood shaking for a moment, until Vanzetti prompted him: 'Anybody else?'

'Uh . . .' Hans forced his hands open again and rubbed his forehead giddily. 'Well, Dr Satamori, and Dr Pech, and I also had a few words with Dr Ingrid Castelnuovo, and – '

'That'll do very well. I shall have to ask for a word of confirmation, just for the record, but nothing more.'

'All done,' the doctor said, putting away his gear. 'We can finish the job at the morgue.'

'Good, thank you.' Vanzetti hesitated. 'Mr Dykstra, would you rather come with us now and make a statement, or wait until you've recovered a bit from the shock?'

'Oh, I'd rather get it out of the way,' Hans sighed. 'I wouldn't want to try and catch some sleep, the state I'm in. I'd have nightmares, I'm sure of it.'

It went smoothly, click-click as designed. Make the statement; agree to attend the inquest tomorrow morning; call in to his headquarters office, saying he wouldn't be available for work; hear that Boris Pech had been among the lucky ones who survived the bloodbath at Aleuker's, and was in hospital but conscious and willing to confirm that Hans had been present . . .

No least hint from anybody of anything but genuine sympathy for a man who had tragically lost that ultra-precious commodity, a legally-married wife.

'And will you go back home now?' Vanzetti asked solicit-ously. 'Or would you rather spend some time elsewhere, with friends perhaps?'

Hans shook his head. 'I'd rather be alone. I guess maybe I shall go call on one or two people who knew Dany par-ticularly well, break the news to them personally . . . If you can't reach me at home, that's what I'll be doing, but I shan't stay away for more than a few hours at a time.'

'Oh, it's most unlikely we shall want to contact you,' Vanzetti said with a casual wave. 'Just so long as you're on time at the inquest . . . Goodbye for the moment, then.'

Hans forced a mechanical smile and headed for the skelter. At its threshold he stopped dead.

'Is something wrong?' Vanzetti called.

'I – I . . . Yes, I just realized something is horribly wrong. It's getting through to me. I felt all numb at first – I guess maybe I threw up my emotions, in a weird kind of way . . . But I shall have to move house. I mean, if next month, or next year, I suddenly think: I punched this code and there was – was Dany . . . ' He swallowed loudly. 'Do you know anything about what turns people into stucks? Because I just got this flash about becoming one myself, if I don't move away from Valletta.'

'Hmm! Yes, I can well believe it,' Vanzetti said. 'You ought to talk to your friend Dr Bonetti about that, don't you think?'

'Yes. Yes, you're quite right, and I shall.'

But not right now. Not today. Today was for being at Anneliese's side when she awoke, symbol of the stability and reassurance she craved and had not received from Chaim Aleuker.

Also it would be for figuring out where to make his new home, out of all the thousands of places the skelter could take him to.

With his new wife.

87

It was no cynical creator who forbade us
to water the deserts and feed the hungry mouths.

You stood with a loaf and a bomb in either hand
and kept the loaf and gave the bomb away.

You chose to have more and even drier deserts
and many mouths will not again taste hunger.

— MUSTAPHA SHARIF

Chapter 13

Drowsing at last after thinking long and hard about what
he had said concerning Aleuker's plan, Mustapha woke to
the frantic shout of Ali at his bedroom door.

'Effendi! It is Dr Satamori who came back! His head is
cut and he is bleeding!'

On the instant Mustapha was wide awake, wondering
whether it was time for him to admit that he believed in
premonitions. He shouted orders for Satamori to receive
medical attention, and minutes later joined him in the Room
of Flowers where he lay stretched on a hand-carved couch,
eyes closed, face a mask of pain, clothes ragged and smeared
with dirt and blood.

'Fred!' Mustapha cried. 'What happened to you?'

Wincing now and then as a boy armed with a box bearing
the sign of the Red Crescent attended to his injuries, Satamori forced out a brief account of the disaster which had
overtaken Aleuker's party. Mustapha hissed in dismay.

'You think Chaim himself is among the dead?'

'I don't think – I know. I saw him killed by a ricocheting
slug. It tore him open and spilled his guts on the floor. Like
ripping a paper sack of butcher's meat!'

'We have lost, then, a very precious man,' Mustapha said heavily.

'Oh, don't strike poses!' Satamori snapped. 'I know you detested him as much as me! I know you were sure he was forever doing the absolutely wrong thing!'

'No, that's untrue,' Mustapha said, feeling for and settling himself on a stool which he could draw close to the couch. 'A man who had once seen the correct thing to do, and done it, must be regarded differently from those who never thought of anything new. At any moment he might have done something just as useful as inventing the privateer. Now that chance has vanished forever.'

'I'm too sick and tired to bother with your doubletalk,' Satamori sighed. 'But – but thank you anyway, for taking me in.'

'My friend, I am flattered that you came to me!' Mustapha exclaimed. 'Did you not have the chance to tell others they would be welcome here?'

'Ah . . . no. No chance at all. There was panic. It started as soon as the Maoris attacked. In fact – oh, it's ironical, in a way – the first person to arrive was the first to turn and run. I mean, apart from those who were invited to show up ahead of time, like Boris Pech and myself.'

'Hmm! You mean you lost all benefit from this treasure-hunt party? You don't know who it was who first unriddled your clues and found his way to Chaim's house?'

'Oh, no! It was a recuperator called Hans Dykstra, who lives in Valletta, I believe. I was lying flat on the floor along with everybody else because one of the first shots smashed a wall-high window and there was glass flying all over the room, but I turned my head away and that's how I happened to see him rush for the skelter. And not by himself, either. Did you hear about this girl Chaim rescued a while ago from the wilds of Brazil? Dykstra was talking to her all by himself for most of the evening, and they were sitting right near the skelter, and he literally dragged her away with him. It would have been funny if it hadn't been so tragic.'

There followed a long silence during which the boy with the first-aid kit completed his task and left the room.

Eventually Mustapha said, 'Rest now, Frederick. Stay and sleep where you are. Ali will make sure that someone watches by you until you waken. After a rest you will certainly feel better.'

'Thank you,' Satamori mumbled, and rolled on his side and passed out almost on the instant.

It was not until he was safely clear of the Room of Flowers that Mustapha dared give way to the sense of terror which had exploded in his belly on hearing Satamori's news.

Hans Dykstra! First to arrive at Aleuker's party! Singled out as though he were the chance member of a crowd on whom a brilliant spotlight fell, the computer-chosen winner of a lottery!

Of all the billion people left on earth, no one more dangerous could have been successful in the treasure-hunt.

Worse yet, he had escaped – started the panic, if Satamori could be believed, and dragged along with him this girl nicknamed Barbara, and . . .

And something must be done at once, for security's sake.

Would he have gone home? Logically, yes . . . but to a chilly welcome. Mustapha had met and evaluated Dany. Chatting with her once, for about ten minutes, had given him a complete picture of her personality. If her husband came back from a party held by somebody as famous as Chaim Aleuker, which she would doubtless have wanted to attend herself, and brought with him a girl in her teens, allegedly very pretty, then there would be hell and all its devils let loose.

So if he had any shred of his wits about him, Hans would not have gone back to Malta. Where else, then . . . ?

Ah. Yes, quite conceivably. That code, after all, would have been at the forefront of his mind, ready to hand when the attack began. And on that skelter there was no privateer, and . . .

It would take only a few minutes to confirm his guess. Mustapha hastened up the staircase of his tallest minaret, entered the secret room containing his third skelter, put on his climatized clothing, and punched the code for the Eriksson house at Umeå.

Hans had been so sure – so absolutely certain – that there would be no one in the Swedish house apart from Anneliese, that for the first several seconds after his return he thought only of trivia. The sun had gone down after the brief northern winter day, but it was warm, therefore the heating system must be working okay because the fire had died to embers. Beside it in the gloom a cloaked figure sat, logically Anneliese wrapped in a blanket, and he hoped she had not woken so long before he arrived that she was frightened and –

And the last chunk of a log slipped on the hearth and uttered a spirt of bright yellow flame. The light revealed that the person waiting for him was not Anneliese.

He exploded with mingled rage and terror.

'Mustapha! What the hell are you doing here? You've broken our compact!'

'It is not my custom to resort to the *tu quoque*,' Mustapha murmured. 'If it were, I might well say that you not only broke it, but smashed it into fragments and trampled those fragments into dust. Must I remind you that I laid it down as a condition of supplying you with illegal codes that you should never under any circumstances bring another person to one of these abandoned homes?'

'What other person am I supposed to have brought?' Hans cried, knowing even as he voiced the words that they were futile.

Mustapha clucked with his tongue: tsk-tsk. 'Though I'm blind I am not unaware of what goes on around me,' he retorted. 'You of all people should have realized that by now. I scented the girl the moment I left the skelter, over and through the smoke of the fire which doubtless you built for her. And, by the way, keep your voice down. She slept contentedly throughout my inspection of her, but she is near to waking and a loud noise may rouse her.'

'Your – inspection?' Hans forced out, advancing on Mustapha with fists clenched. 'You've been *feeling* her?'

'Oh, I was right! I sense jealousy!' Mustapha said. 'I was unaware that she had become your property . . . ? I have no eyesight, man, but my fingertips – you saw – are delicate enough to stroke the full length of a spider-web and leave it unbroken. You think to touch a girl is to maul her, ravish her; I think of it as having to be lighter than a glance. She did not even turn over, let alone wake up . . . How old is she, this girl whom Chaim retrieved from the Brazilian *sertão*? Seventeen? Eighteen?'

'Who told you . . . ?' Hans's voice failed him in mid-question.

'I was right again,' Mustapha said. 'You imagined your departure with her from Aleuker's home was unobserved. You are too commonplace, too *interchangeable* a person to sense that unique recognizes unique. I am not surprised that you found your way to Chaim's party. I am surprised that Chaim and his friends imagined that people like you could save the world, frozen as you are into the mold of the past. You're like a vampire, one of the undead, compelled to spend half his life in a coffin.'

Blood was roaring in Hans's ears, and the room swayed and swirled. He said, 'Okay, so someone saw me leave Aleuker's with her, but I may well have saved her life by bringing her here and –'

'Here? Instead of Valletta? Most people in the grip of panic think at once of going home.' Mustapha's tone was gentle enough, but contempt rode the edge of his words as light may ride the sharpness of a knife-blade. 'Not of course that you could have made it clear to your wife that your intention was simply to save the life of a poor friendless girl –'

Grasping at a straw, Hans rapped, 'Of course not! You've met her, you can imagine what a scene she'd have created!'

Mustapha shook his head. 'Wrong reason, and dishonest with it.'

'What?'

'I can read you more clearly than you, with your good eyesight, can read one of the books I've sold you.' Mustapha rose, reaching out one hand to the brick-built side of the chimney that swallowed the small remaining trace of smoke from the fire. 'You could have convinced Dany you'd brought the girl home to save her life, if that had been the truth . . . but it was not. I can hear the processes of your imagination. I can put them into words, even into English words, though I would be more precise and crueller in Arabic. I see your whole plan laid out before me, like a map, like a carved stela from Luxor that my fingers have grown acquainted with. I say this is what you intend!'

He drew himself bolt upright, and his blind eyes seemed to shine dazzlingly into Hans's.

'I say your plan goes like this. You have by chance been brought together with a girl who is lost in the modern world. Aleuker, a busy man, with more friends, more women, more preoccupations than he could cope with, neglected her when he found her childhood conditioning had scarred her mind too deeply for her to be turned into a decent citizen of today's world.

'But you have the time, and the urge. Hating your wife, possessing her not as a person and a partner but as a trophy, a prize that all too many men these days can never aspire to, you suddenly realize there's a chance for you to supplant her. What likelier target than a girl who's lonely and miserable and frightened? In a few months, gratitude; in a year or so, divorce – Dany like any other woman can always find an eager youth wanting to share her bed – and after that marriage, legal binding marriage, with a teenage girl who's been carefully prevented from involving herself with anybody except Hans Dykstra. It won't be love, but you never understood what love is. You want to buy this child, as though she were a slave, and bind her to you with intangible chains.'

The diagnosis was too terribly accurate for Hans to answer at once. He gulped air, swayed, blinked, at last found his voice again.

'You dare to say that to me? You, who've done the same and worse to kids from all over the world? Spent your time and money hunting for orphans, boys as well as girls so long as they're pretty and bright, seduced them into your bed and imprisoned them in your home and taught them just those jobs they can't make use of anywhere else if they do decide to try and escape from you? What do you pay for the children *you* enslave?'

'I pay what you can't because you never had any,' Mustapha said, and the words quavered unexpectedly. A glint from the fire showed, bewilderingly, that tears had gathered in his sightless eyes, and now of a sudden they spilled over and ran down his face.

'What? What?'

'I pay love.' The poet gathered himself again, brushed

93

at his itching cheeks. 'I have never fettered any of my protégés. Of either sex. I have kissed and embraced and comforted those who never before in their lives were touched by another person except to be punched or slapped. I have broken my heart so many times it is held together with rivets like a shattered porcelain bowl, because I have always let go those I loved with the depths of my being when they said it was time for them to become themselves, to be individuals and not to depend on me any more. Compared to what you plan to make of this girl – a bunch of reflexes, a machine whose buttons you can press at will – I am sinless and without reproach.'

The world turned red around Hans. Without volition he snatched at a poker lying on the side of the hearth, hot but not too hot to grasp, and used it to silence that accusing tongue.

Proverbially
'Absence makes the heart grow fonder'
– Or so said they who are no longer with us.

Likewise however
'To be out of sight is to be out of mind'
– I never knew which proverb to believe.

You whom I love
Stepped through the skelter yesterday.
– Now I have had proof that both are true.

> – MUSTAPHA SHARIF

Chapter 14

'Who – ? Hans! What – ? Oh, *God* . . . !'

An incredible confusion of slump, cry, run, exclaim, moan. It all happened in a time when he was out of touch with the universe; it sandwiched together, compressed, declined to be separated again.

But that was a moment ago. This moment: Anneliese at the door of the room where she had been sleeping, staring at what the wan firelight showed, petrified by horror. Her dress was crumpled, and in a sense so was her face, for she had been lying on a fold in the pillows and a deep dent marked her left cheek like a sort of brand.

Nobody, no matter how dull-witted, could have failed to add together a scene like this: prone by the hearth, a stranger unconscious, dark blood trickling out of his hair, and Hans still clutching the poker he had struck out with.

He remained in a daze until she managed to utter the all-important question: 'Have you -- *killed* him?'

'No, no!' Hans's mind seemed to rush back into normal operation; he could think again, discovered a cluster of excuses full-blown and ready for use.

'Who is he?'

'I've no idea. But I know what he is.'

She advanced a pace toward him, hands clenched, jaw-muscles lumping as though to restrain a scream, and waited for him to elaborate.

Now I've got to pile yet another untruth atop the crazy pyramid I've already erected. Why? Why? How did I get tangled in this lunatic mess? I lost my temper, that's all – first with Dany, then with Mustapha, both times with complete justification. And all of a sudden it turns out I'm snarled up as though I've been wrapped in barbed wire!

Was I to know so many people would notice me leaving Aleuker's that Mustapha would get to hear in a matter of hours?

Oh, maybe I should have guessed. After all, I bought notoriety, didn't I? By being the person who won Boris Pech his bet . . .

I'm not myself. It's all happened too fast. I claim to follow the Way of Life and I just used frenzied violence against a fellow human being. That's not like me. It isn't – I'm sure it isn't in my real nature to do that!

So I'll be justified if I put the best possible light on things. I'll atone later. When I've straightened matters out. After the inquest on Dany. After finding somewhere to live a long, long way away from Malta. I can just disappear from the awareness of my friends. My colleagues at work must be informed, naturally . . . but I can lose the people who knew me with Dany, I can start over somehow, I can –

The rush of thought had to break off. Anneliese was staring at him, still waiting for the reply to her last question.

He fumbled for the proper words.

'I'm dreadfully sorry about this. But I imagine you've been told there are still criminals in our modern world?'

'Y-yes . . . ' Her voice was as faint as autumn wind.

'This is one. Of the worst kind. What we call a code-breaker. A person who figures out how to use a private skelter, and sneaks in to rob people's homes, and if he's caught to kill the person who catches him.'

'Are you sure?'

'Do you think I'd use this' – brandishing the poker – 'if I weren't?'

'I thought I heard you talking together,' she ventured.

'Well – well, of course! I wouldn't have knocked him down on sight, would I? But when he couldn't give a satisfactory account of his presence . . . Well, there was only one sensible course of action.'

'I . . . ' She shook her head. 'I must have misunderstood. I believed that because of something Chaim invented, this didn't happen anymore. Didn't he devise what they call a privateer?'

Hans cursed silently. Ignorant this girl might be; she was in no sense stupid.

'Yes, but I'm talking about the sort of burglar who can get around a privateer. What one man can invent, another can evade. It's very rare, but it does happen now and then.'

'I – I see.'

'There are always flaws in the best of systems. You get transmission errors, for example, like the one which – ' He interrupted himself, momentarily experiencing a renewal of his former panic. The less often Anneliese was reminded about the 'anonymous' dead woman, the better.

'But I've got to get you out of here.'

'What? Why?'

'Because where one code-breaker gets in, another may follow. Very often they work in gangs. If this one doesn't report back in half an hour or so, his confederates may very likely come to see what's happened . . . You poor girl! It must be absolutely terrible to have seen so much of what's bad in today's world, and so little of what's good. I do promise you, it is possible to be happy and enjoy yourself and make plans for the future and see them fulfilled. I want to give you that. You deserve it.'

In memory, an echo of Mustapha's accusations . . . but he stifled it.

'Where will you take me, then?'

'A safe place. Just for long enough to sort this out. I shall have to tell the police, of course, and then I'll have to have the skelter re-coded. It takes a few hours. I'm so sorry, I really am! Because what I most want to be doing is help you. You – ah – you don't mind my wanting to help you?'

All the color drained from her cheeks.

'Hans, where would I be if there wasn't somebody to help me? I could be dead! Couldn't I?'

Marvelous! Oh, *marvelous*!

Hans opened his arms just in time as she rushed at him and buried her face in his shoulder and convulsed into sobs.

There followed an unmeasured period during which she wept and he caressed her back through one thin layer of cloth and dreamed of the time when the cloth would no longer be there. How long would it take to persuade her, by slow degrees, that it was okay for her to strip in his presence?

Too soon. Too soon! Keep your head, Hans Dykstra, and don't push your luck.

Eventually he drew back from her and murmured something about having to hurry. She nodded pliantly.

'Just to be on the safe side,' he said, 'I guess I'd better tie this villain up so he can't get away before the police collect him – '

'You will not send for them at once? They could be waiting here when his confederates come, couldn't they?'

Once more Hans chided himself for underestimating this girl's native wit. How to get around that little problem – ?

Ah.

'But suppose the police and the other code-breakers arrive together! You could be involved in another gunfight! You just escaped from one at Aleuker's – surely you don't want to risk another? Just do as I say, and everything will work out fine!'

She raised no more objections, and within another five minutes they entered the skelter together and he pressed the code for a Way of Life refuge he had once visited in Bali. Anneliese might be disturbed at finding herself among committed heathens; still, the place had three great advantages. They took in anybody, gave help and never asked too many questions; they were always extremely busy and maintained no records, preferring to get on with their real work and forget about what happened yesterday; and very few

people there spoke more than a smattering of English, let
alone Flemish or *Plattdütsh.*

They were received at the skelter door by a smiling, thirtyish
woman garlanded with flowers; flowers were also braided
into her black hair. Apart from that, she wore only a sort
of kilt secured with a belt of woven leather from which
dangled a small pouch. Anneliese's fingers cramped painfully
on Hans's arm as she realized that by her standards the
woman was shamelessly unclad.

He murmured reassuringly, 'You probably find this hard
to believe . . . but you're looking at a nun.'

She turned wide disbelieving eyes to him. 'A – a *nun*?'
she repeated.

'What else do you call someone who has decided to
dedicate her existence to helping others because of what
she believes?'

'I . . . ' Anneliese's voice failed her. Just as well; it would
have complicated matters beyond bearing to try and fill in
the details. A somewhat more exact term than 'nun' might
have been 'temple prostitute' – but it would still have been
wide of the mark. The concepts of the Way of Life were
as subtle as any evolved by previous religions, and required
a very open mind.

By then, however, the woman was making them welcome
with smiles, and for each of them a posy of fresh-picked
flowers – which went a long way to assuaging Anneliese's
alarm – and inviting them with gestures to leave the small
room in which the skelter was located and follow her down
a quiet corridor walled with stone and lit at intervals with
lamps set behind translucent paintings, all of various living
organisms, from naked athletes to lowly bacteria shown
magnified thousands of times.

'It is the belief of these people that no harm should
ever be done to any evolved creature,' Hans whispered.
'With one exception: if a superior creature may be saved
from suffering thereby. They are willing to cure diseases
even though it means killing germs – you follow me? –
provided a human life can be made better because of it.
You'll find them very kind and very generous. This is a
refuge which they keep open for anybody who wants to

come to it: people for whom life is too much of a problem, who need to rest and relax and think things out, or people who are ill and have no friends or relatives to look after them . . . You don't have to believe what they believe. They give what they can and leave it at that.'

'I – I see,' Anneliese answered. 'Once I read a book about monks at the Pass of St Bernard in Switzerland, who had to help everybody lost in the snow. Is it like that?'

'Yes, very like. Except you should say: people lost in the world.'

He was infinitely relieved to find her so open-minded. Doubtless she would also be favorably impressed when she learned that no meat was ever eaten here because no follower of the Way of Life could kill an animal – he himself had never become a convert to total vegetarianism, but he had often had qualms of conscience about it. When it came to some of the rituals glorifying sensuality, on the other hand, Anneliese might well be completely repelled . . . but with luck she would have to stay here so short a time, she wouldn't even hear rumors about that side of it.

To an elderly, likewise nearly naked, woman of perhaps sixty who had retained an astonishingly attractive figure even though her face was wrinkled like an old apple – but wrinkled for the right reason, because she had talked and smiled and laughed a great deal all her life – he explained slowly in English the reason why he had brought Anneliese here. He referred to her parents' fate, and then to the attack at Aleuker's, and then to the burglar at his home where he'd taken her for safety, and the elderly woman nod-nodded every time she got the picture through the barrier of a half-comprehended language.

'We shall help and take care,' she said firmly. 'Is a badness, so much hate and hurt. Will here be safe!'

He asked Anneliese, 'Do you think you can stand it here for a while, as long as it takes me to sort everything out?'

She bit her lip.

'I think so,' she said. 'I don't understand why these people do what they do, but it must always be good to help people in trouble, I think. I don't really understand why you're helping me, either, but I am very grateful to you.'

That encouraged him to embrace her on parting, and even

100

to plant a chaste kiss on her lips: light, very brotherly, most out of keeping with the practices of the Way of Life . . . but luckily Anneliese didn't notice the look of astonished disapproval that crossed the face of the old nun.

He was humming as he stepped back through the skelter in Sweden, rehearsing the terms of the bargain he was going to strike with Mustapha: leave me alone, and I won't report you for selling illegal codes. Fair?

It would have been. Would have *had* to be.

But Mustapha had disappeared.

The great courtesans
Reported by old scandalmongers
Notched up their respectable collections
Of noblemen and servants and friends
But never managed
Because they could not manage
What girls of the most respectable descent
Take for granted in modern times –
That they should sleep
In seven beds on seven continents
Incontinently in any given week. . . .

– MUSTAPHA SHARIF

Chapter 15

In the other of the two rooms of his home where nobody except his closest and most intimate servants entered – the first being the room with his secret skelter, the second *not* being his bedroom which had been shared over the years with an amazing range of partners – Mustapha Sharif waved aside with thanks that same boy who had tended Satamori's wounds and pronounced himself capable of thinking clearly again.

Ali and Feisal, his body-servants, and Muley the chief scribe who was the third of his right hands – he had created that conceit for a poem, long ago – stood about him, exuding anxiety so fiercely he did not need eyes to read their expressions.

'It must be done as it was done before,' Muley said in a sententious voice.

'No.' Mustapha rubbed his forehead; his head still ached, but a cold compress and a salve and a glass of sweet mint tea with a pain-killing drug dissolved in it had brought his body's agony under control. He said again, 'No, not in any detail the way it was done before. Instead of dealing solely with a conscious criminal, we now have to take steps to ensure the safety of an innocent girl, barely more than a child, for whom this – this *person* has conceived a fate worse than imprisonment. He plans to put shackles on her mind, cripple her in a way which no bodily restraint could match. He is moreover unaware of what evil he is hatching . . . Muley, I trust you as I trust myself, and sometimes more so. Judge in accordance with what you believe a man who is married, who chose a woman older than himself, not altogether intelligent, confined her to him by legal bonds, made her so miserable that she learned how to hate him and herself too, and on the basis of a spur-of-the-moment encounter, attained by sheer chance, decided he was going to abandon her – knowing, admittedly, that any woman still capable of standing, sitting, lying and spreading her legs is instantly desirable nowadays – but regardless of that reservation is *capable* of discarding her because he has a chance of deluding an ignorant teenage girl into the misconception that she must depend on him and him alone in order to keep afloat in a world she doesn't understand . . . Well?'

Muley plucked at his large lower lip; he was a portly man, full-jowled, pot-bellied, soft . . . because when he was a very small boy he had trodden on an inefficient anti-personnel mine, which did not kill him but did reduce him to a condition that in other ages had been more deliberately created. He also limped on his left leg.

'I already passed my judgement,' he said. 'Before you set forth those facts. Because there is one additional fact you seem not to have heard.'

'Tell me, then!'

'This man is not married. He is widowed.'

Mustapha tensed. 'Explain, explain! How do you know?'

'The moment you returned, on the basis of what you were able to mumble through your pain, I initiated an inquiry – discreetly, by roundabout routes, but rapidly too. It was not a difficult task. News of an inquest is come by very simply.'

'But you can't be implying that he killed his wife?'

'Indeed, no. The news runs that his wife killed herself as a result of some insult or affront he gave her.'

'Ay-ay-ay!' Mustapha clenched his hands into knobbly soft fists. 'And there is to be an inquest?'

'Tomorrow at 10 a.m. local in the Valletta coroner's court.'

'He is obliged to attend?'

'Yes indeed; he is the only witness to the facts.'

'Oh, but this is a disaster!' Mustapha cried. 'For him not to appear: that will create a planetary hue and cry! But if he does appear, he may let slip something which . . . Yes, it would be fatally easy for him to lose track of his complicated lies.'

'We must eliminate him,' Ali grunted. 'We can catch him when he arrives to attend the court –'

'Out of the question. He has secret files to be opened in the event of his death, recording his expeditions with me, and while he pledged that he would not include any hint of my identity, he may now have gone back on his word.' Mustapha shook his head. 'No, I see only one possibility. We must track him down and persuade him it is still to his advantage to keep our secret. All being well, the threat of a bracelet will fetter his mind more securely than the ropes he used on me!' Mustapha rubbed his chafed wrists and ankles. 'Sometimes, you know, I feel that those with sight overestimate the advantages they derive from it. One would never have believed that anybody in his right mind could do such a sloppy job of lashing a man's arms and legs. In pain, giddy, frightened, I released myself from his amateurish bonds in – oh – perhaps two or three minutes. He left slack on both my wrists, as though he conceived them to be circular instead of twice as thick one way as the other . . . Muley, detach a hundred apprentices and juniors, preferably active and intelligent youths, and assign them to me for instructions. It should not be very hard to pre-guess someone like Hans Dykstra, gripped by fear that prevents him thinking clearly. There are only half a dozen places apart from the Valletta court where we stand a chance of catching him; we should be able to cover all those skelters.'

'We should ambush him at the house in Sweden,' Ali said.

'If there is time – No, I can't imagine that he will have taken until now to discover that I've made my escape. Upon which, if I read his personality aright, he'll smash or burn the place. Not that I'm certain. He's disintegrating. He has now lost both the things that justified his existence in his own eyes, marked him out as more than a member of a mob. He will no longer dare to indulge his illegal hobby, which he engaged in more from bravado than from love of knowledge, and equally he has lost that rare prize, a wife, just at the time when he believed he was about to do what scarcely a man alive today has been able to do – get rid of her in favor of another younger and far more beautiful . . . He has been to a high place and seen the kingdoms of the world. It was all a cheat. He must be losing his mind more from frustration than any other single cause.'

He folded his hands with an air of finality, but the servants made no move to depart.

'Is something still more amiss than you've told me already?'

'There is the matter of Dr Satamori,' Ali said. 'He is still here. Asleep, fortunately . . . but when he wakes he will no doubt wish to express his thanks for your help.'

'Then he must have the chance to do so. But make it clear when he does wake and asks to speak with me that I would far prefer to be at work on a new poem.'

The air in the Eriksson house felt as stiff as glass. When Hans contrived to take a pace forward from the skelter he half-expected to find it crashing down on him, like a shattered dome.

It was still very dark here, but that same log which had flared to reveal Mustapha last time he arrived was conserving a bright glow, and – perhaps fanned by the air which had accompanied his emergence – now transmitted flame to a sort of snake-like object lying in the hearth.

Rope. No doubt the rope Mustapha had been bound with.

Who – *who* – could have come and set the captive free? Had Mustapha guessed he'd be attacked? Had he told one of his many servants, 'If I don't return after such a time, I can be found at such a code and I'll be in trouble'?

Hans put his hands giddily to his temples. Never in all his life had he foreseen he might wind up in a plight like this. It was infinitely worse than the nightmares which he had sometimes experienced as a result of remembering how dangerous his illegal hobby was. Even if he had been braced for it, he had always deep down imagined that there would be people who paradoxically respected him as a martyr. The people he had met at Aleuker's, above all, might have exhibited that response. Surely someone like Boris Pech, who had asked to have a particular item searched out among the garbage of Europe in much the same way as Karl Bonetti, surely he and those he regarded as friends would be tolerant of a selfless infringement of an arbitrarily absolute rule ...

But he wasn't dealing with Pech, Satamori or Castelnuovo. He was dealing with Mustapha Sharif: an unpredictable man, an emotional man, and as much of a stranger as when he and Hans first became acquainted.

In sum: a man whose motives defied scrutiny as completely as if he were insane.

After only a few seconds of struggle, Hans realized that it was useless to try and reason his way out of yet another crisis before he slept. His day had been stretched to more than double its normal length; he was shaking more from weariness than fear – after all, he had produced inspired solutions already to several seemingly insoluble problems – and in a few hours he must really have all his wits about him. Checking his watch, he was appalled to see just how little time did remain before he was required to report for Dany's inquest.

Nonetheless he felt a need as deep as hunger to *do* something, at once. It was as though the sort of fury which wrenches the power to act from the head down to the guts had been grafted on to his conscious mind; he felt a blending of naked anger with dazzling insight.

'It will teach him a lesson!' he said to the air. 'It will show him I'm not to be trifled with, even though I am a lowly recuperator and not a world-famous public figure!'

He strode forward across the floor, suddenly released from his moment of subjective paralysis.

By the bed where Anneliese had slept, the candle he had set ready, and the matches. He lit the candle and carried it back into the living-zone, trailing also the duvet, the big feather-stuffed coverlet, under which the girl had lain and which was – he fancied – a little scented with her body.

He went into the kitchen, and there opened the cock on the side of the oil-tank serving the central heating system. He soaked the duvet, then dragged it across the floor after

106

him so that there was a thick line of oil on the floor, thick enough to catch light and feed flame back to the puddle accumulating alongside the tank. Once the candle was touched to it, the whole lot would go up in a great smoky bonfire.

At the last moment, instead of simply tossing the candle at the duvet and stepping into the skelter, he checked. He had never heard of a means to inactivate a skelter by remote control . . . but suppose Mustapha had arranged things so that he was meant to be trapped here? Suppose the elderly skelter had been sabotaged? He could burn to death in his own fire!

He thought about that for a while, with a very clear and detached attitude, weighing the pros and cons. Eventually he balanced the candle on a candlestick, about eight or nine centimeters high, and leaned the duvet against it and used a folded shred of paper as a sort of fuse, certain to catch within five minutes but no sooner.

Candle burns down while paper soaks up a little oil – paper burns and falls on duvet – duvet blazes up and the tank explodes . . . Right.

He entered the skelter. It worked perfectly. He was at home. With a sigh of relief he half-expected to make the walls shake, he rushed into his own bedroom – that had been shared with Dany – set his alarm, and collapsed into sleep without bothering to undress.

O my friend you have come a long way
from your home in the next town north –
  sit and take refreshment.

O my enemy you have come no distance
from your home the other side of Earth –
  speak and at once be gone.

            – Mustapha Sharif

Chapter 16

The building where the coroner's inquest was to be held had
been a hotel during the period when Malta was a popular
tourist resort. It had been damaged in a riot and patched
in an extraordinary fashion, by an architect who was a
devoted Maltese nationalist and felt it insulting to have
'modern' buildings on this island. Even before its floors and
windows had been mended, even before they fixed the
damage due to fire-bombs and bullets, he had insisted they
disguise its frontage with more 'traditional' decoration. So,
where there had been balconies of plain concrete and pre-
cast iron rails, there were now rain-worn plaster copies of
the kind of molding seen on ancient churches, some threatening to break loose and needing to be lashed in place with bits
of wire.

  But after the Blowup most people had kept their heads
even less well than that architect.

Hans's mouth was dry, and his eyes were blurred because
despite setting his alarm he had overslept and left home in
such a hurry he had forgotten to bring his dark glasses. It
was a bright sunny day.

At least, however, what had haunted him during his short sleep and filled his dream with images of distilled terror had not come to pass. They were not making a grand scandal out of the death of this married woman, even though the circumstances were scandalous. There were newspapers here, because the TV was under-funded and unreliable, and in the ancient manner they were sold on the streets by people who could find no better employment: notably by bracees.

On the placards held by those he passed as he walked to the court, however, he read the day's headlines, and all were concerned with the tragedy at Aleuker's party; there had been arrests in the local Maori community, and some whites had been accused of complicity, and enough really important, really famous people had been killed to make that the chief topic of discussion the world around.

Call it a fringe benefit. Time was when an event like Dany's suicide, because of its local connections, would have displaced whatever happened half a world away, up to and possibly including the scale of an outbreak of war. Thanks to (*thanks* to . . . !) influenza-M, Alaskan croup and a particularly virulent strain of cholera, the Maltese population had been slashed by seventy per cent, had become too small to run the islands properly, had had to be topped up by bribed immigration. The device had been used before, and came readily to mind.

So this morning he had only a minor ordeal to face. He would testify in exactly the same terms as he had employed when confronted by Vanzetti, he would benefit from the sympathy of the court because he had lost that precious and all-too-often irreplaceable asset, his wife, and that would be that. By lunchtime or thereabout he'd be able to head for the Balinese refuge, collect Anneliese (before she was overexposed to the ideals of the Way of Life, a sniggering demon remarked from the corner of his mind – but that was untrue and irrelevant anyhow!), and ask her where on the planet she would most like to live. Ah, a great idea. Invoke her opinion from the very start, that was the ticket. Make sure she was emotionally committed to everything from this day forward. In next to no time she would be taking it for granted that he and she did everything together, including choosing a home. So the right course would be to indent for compassionate leave from his job, which of course would be granted without demur, and spend the next week or two getting well acquainted and exploring some of the likeliest locations for their new home, and –

He had just realized that he was humming cheerfully, and that was wholly wrong for a man whose wife had died under such circumstances, when he rounded the last corner on the way to the building where the court was to meet for the inquest.

And stopped dead.

He had only been that one time to Mustapha's palace at Luxor. But he remembered with the clarity of a hallucinogen dream the features of the chief scribe, Muley Hassan, who had shown him over the scriptorium.

He was here. In ordinary European clothing instead of his regular Egyptian garb – not that that would have excited comment in Valletta, there being a very high proportion of Arabs in the modern Maltese population – with dark glasses on his nose . . . but unmistakable as he glanced at his watch as though confirming the time of arrival of a friend with whom he had a long-standing appointment.

Hans stepped back as though he had been physically pushed. A person behind – he wasn't paying enough attention to his surroundings to tell if it was a man or woman, but he did recognize: very fat and wheezing – complained in a volley of curses, mixed English-Arabic-Maltese with a crowning splotch of obscene German.

'But I mustn't miss the inquest!' Hans breathed to the uncaring crowds about him.

So . . . what about a back entry? Perhaps one where he could contact one of the helpful policemen he'd had such sympathy from?

He thought very hard about the layout of this district, and concluded that there was a back route which would cost only a few minutes, and – oh, miracle! Glimpsed through a door about to slam shut, perhaps a service door when this was a hotel, that same sergeant who had first appeared in his skelter and recorded the deposition about permitting the police to enter his home!

He rushed forward shouting, and the man responded by holding the door ajar.

'Mr Dykstra! You ought to be in court by now!' he exclaimed.

'I know, I know, and I'm trying to get there.' Lies flowed from Hans's tongue more smoothly than oil; the habit was becoming compulsive. 'But I'm trying to avoid somebody who knew Dany and – and I guess thinks it was my fault and I'm scared!'

The sergeant looked grim. 'Ah. I know just what you mean. We've had half a dozen cases like that. You're talking about the sort of person who thinks every time a woman dies the race is in greater danger than it was yesterday?'

It was the first time Hans had heard of people who held such opinions, but they jibed magnificently with the spur-of-the-moment invention he'd contrived. He nodded.

'Right. Come with me. I'll have a word with Chief Vanzetti. If we have to, we can always clear the court.'

'Oh, I hope that won't be necessary,' Hans said, and could hear how sanctimonious his voice had become. 'Although I guess it *might* be a good idea . . .'

The judge was convinced it was a good idea immediately. He was a testy man oozing perspiration like pork oozing fat as it turns on a spit.

'I will not tolerate the slightest risk of a disturbance in my court!' he barked. 'If this unfortunate Mr Dykstra is liable to be hounded by lunatics . . . ! Is there any doubt that we have a simple suicide?'

Vanzetti shook his head. 'According to our forensic people it all hangs together perfectly.'

'In camera, then!' the judge said. 'I know the press won't like it, but they may go jump in the sea for all I care, I'm overworked and underpaid and I wish *I* had time to pursue crackpot notions too!'

The whole inquest, in the near-silence of a large and almost empty room which must originally have been a banquet-hall, lasted under half an hour, and closed with the judge expressing his condolences.

Leaving the room in company with Vanzetti, Hans said diffidently, 'Chief Inspector, you've been tremendously kind,

111

but I wonder if I might impose on your good will just a little longer . . . ?'

'What? Oh, by all means, I'll do what I can for you. Do you want help in re-registering your domicile or something? I recall your saying you were afraid of becoming a stuck if you had to keep coming back to the same place where your wife died, and I must admit if something like that happened to me I'd be equally upset.'

'Uh . . . well, more or less,' Hans said with a swift change of mental gears. 'I'm not sure where I want to move to yet, but I do know I'd like to stay out of sight of certain – ah – fanatics.'

'Do you know how you attracted their attention?'

'Uh – no. Unless,' he added quickly as inspiration dawned, 'it has something to do with my making it to Aleuker's party. Perhaps somebody who was cheated of the chance . . . '

'And doesn't realize how lucky he or she was,' Vanzetti grunted. 'You heard the death toll is up to fourteen? Two more of the guests died and they have little hope of saving another two.'

'Shameful! Shameful!'

'Yes, one would have expected mankind to learn a lesson from the Blowup, only . . . ' Vanzetti shrugged. 'Well, it isn't my job to re-design humanity, thanks be. You want access to an official skelter, is that it? Under escort, so nobody can get at you?'

'Yes, please. I'll get my home – my old home – recoded so it can be offered for sale, but until then I think it might be sensible for me to intrude on the hospitality of various friends . . . Will you be needing me again?'

'You heard the verdict. Suicide while of unsound mind. The case is closed.' Vanzetti hesitated. 'I must admit, Mr Dykstra –'

'You're going to say,' Hans interrupted, 'that I could have been a little kinder to my wife. Yes, I guess so. But you know about her mental instability, and Dr Bonetti was kind enough to send that affidavit, and – I did my best. I promise you, my absolute best. It wasn't enough.'

'That's a tough admission for any man to make,' Vanzetti said. 'I think I rather admire you for being able to say it. So often one runs across people who are determined to deny their own inadequacy . . . No, change that to shortcomings. It's more tactful.'

'Either way it hurts like hell,' Hans said. 'I vaguely remember a quotation: "The bell tolls for thee".'

'A favorite of mine, too,' Vanzetti said with a nod. 'I suppose I wound up in police work for that kind of reason. We're all diminished by the stupidity and brutality of any given person, including us. Very well, Mr Dykstra, I'll be glad to ensure you get safely into the skelter system, and we'll keep watch for anybody trying to pester you by using the code for your home until that's revised.'

'Oh, don't go to that much trouble, please!'

'No trouble, none at all!' With an airy wave. 'Codebreakers are among the worst criminals of all, aren't they? And the offense is compounded if what they're trying to do is sneak past the privateer of someone recently bereaved.'

It was getting worse all the time, even when it appeared to be going best! Life was cram-jam-full of lunatic paradoxes all of a sudden, and Hans felt himself being squeezed into new hateful painful shapes as a result, because there was no room in the world for both him and them.

His plea to Vanzetti had succeeded at once . . . but now he was faced with an even worse problem. Believing he was persecuted by madmen, Vanzetti was bringing to bear the force of the law on Hans's predicament . . .

And who had more to fear from the law than himself, the man who had broken code after code for years not by his own skills but by bribing somebody else? It was bribery, the kind of arrangement he'd made with Mustapha; it was conspiracy too, and there were other and even nastier names he shut away to the side of his mind.

It seemed hideously certain that very soon he was going to be – to be *somewhere*, at some random location on the face of the planet, staring at a new neat shiny metal bracelet and thinking how much of his life had been destroyed.

Unless he contrived to salvage something from the wreck.

The image came readily to mind; had he not spent most of his working adulthood salvaging things that other people were then allowed to make use of? Was it not high time that he take advantage of a salvage operation performed by someone else? Was that not the clear incontestable definition of what he in fact was doing?

All these thoughts rushed through his mind as he was whisked away from the court building to the nearby police headquarters and politely invited to step into a secure skelter there, one where no camera or detector could note and record the code punched by a person departing. It was forbidden by law to record that.

Poising his fingers, he spent a final second on confirming his opinion of what he was committed to. Yes, he was acting in accordance with the ideals of a recuperator. His salvage happened to be a living human being; there was no other difference.

He punched for the Way of Life refuge in Bali.

Today is today but
Where is here when it can be
    Everywhere?

Then was then and
Why is now if it can be
    Any time?

I live next to no time and no time
Is an extremely disconcerting neighbor.

                    – MUSTAPHA SHARIF

Chapter 17

He found Anneliese in a plain small room which might have
been the twin of the one in which he himself had slept during
his sole vacation here, before he met Dany. One of its walls
was covered with dark green creeper growing up a wooden
trellis from a shallow pottery tray containing earth. There
was no other decoration.

The girl was dozing on a heap of cushions, partly covered
by a soft pink quilt which on his entrance she gathered
around her body in alarm . . . but not so quickly that he was
unable to glimpse more of her skin than he had so far seen.

He was briefly astonished to notice that it was sickly-
pallid, white as dough. But of course that wasn't to be
wondered at in view of her upbringing. She had probably
never shown her body to the sun. How different from Dany,
who had always assumed that sitting on a beach in the
altogether would instantly conjure up a horde of admiring
men from the sand-dunes.

'Hans, is that you?'

'Yes, of course.' He bent to kiss her cheek; her first impulse
was to flinch away, but she restrained it and suffered his
lips to brush her skin. 'Are you all right?'

115

'Uh . . . ' She sat up cautiously, making certain that the quilt was tightly wrapped about her. 'Yes, they have been kind. They gave me food and drink and took my dress to be laundered.' She hesitated, searching his face with her dark eyes. 'And you? Is everything all right?'

'I'm afraid not.'

'Oh, God! What's gone wrong this time?'

'I think I must have been right about the code-breaker having confederates. The man escaped – and before leaving he set my home on fire.'

'Oh, how horrible! How *horrible!*'

'Yes, it is . . . But perhaps not so horrible as you think.'

'What do you mean?'

He kicked around a cushion and sat down beside her, frowning.

'It's very hard to explain. It's a sort of paradox. I feel – I feel as though I've been set free from something. You remember, when we arrived at my home, I said I'd kept everything as it used to be for far too long?'

'Yes, of course I remember.'

'Now the whole of my past has been so to speak lifted off me. There's nothing I can do about it. It's simply gone. Now, I'm in the same state you were in when you found that Festeburg had been burned.'

'You poor man!' Impulsively, she clasped his nearer hand, almost losing her grip on the quilt . . . but not quite. He curled his fingers around hers, thinking how large and clumsy they were compared to her small cool ones.

'Is it a dreadfully bad thing to have to start one's life again? Isn't it a chance to forget your mistakes and this time get everything right?'

'I . . . ' She bit her lip. 'I suppose if you have a very strong personality, you can look at it that way.'

'I don't think I have a strong personality. But that's the way I'm trying to look at it. Would you like to . . . ?' He hesitated.

'What?'

'Would you like to help me, as I'm helping you? Shall we go together in search of a new place to live, a new life for both of us?'

116

It was a long moment before she answered. It was like a foretaste of eternity.

But in the end she gave a nod and was able to force a smile.

'Wonderful!' Hans cried, and leaned toward her and put his free arm around her shoulders. 'Oh, I thought when I found myself face to face with that inferno I'd die of rage and misery! And here all of a sudden you've made me happier than I imagined possible!'

'Was the house beyond saving when you arrived there?' she whispered.

'Oh, yes. I almost walked into a wall of flames.'

'You didn't hurt yourself?' She released his hand and made to feel his face. 'If it was burning so fiercely –'

'No, I was very quick,' he interrupted. 'I don't believe I even singed my hair. I stayed just long enough to take in the sight, and then I got away at once. I was afraid the skelter might break down with the heat, and strand me. Maybe that was what the criminal intended!'

He felt her shudder, and added hastily, 'Don't distress yourself . . . darling! It's over, over and done with. Let's make our fresh start together right away, and in a few days it will all be as though it never happened. Any idea where you'd like to go? Somewhere sunny and safe, that's what I'd like: the Caribbean, or the Azores, or Polynesia!'

'I – I don't know,' she muttered. 'Those are just noises to me, those names.'

'Then we'll begin by looking them over. It's high time you got acquainted with the planet.' He rose to his feet. 'I'll go find your dress, or if it isn't dry something else that you can wear, and we'll leave at once.'

'You are well rested?' Mustapha inquired solicitously of Dr Satamori. 'You are fully recovered?'

'Well enough to get back to work, certainly,' Satamori said, gingerly touching the neat bandage around his head. 'As for rested . . . I keep having nightmares.'

'It's hardly surprising,' Mustapha murmured. 'I too had a bad dream, concerning what might have happened if I'd gone with you to Chaim's place.'

They walked another few paces along the shady colonnaded pathway leading to the skelter by which Mustapha's guests arrived and left.

Suddenly Satamori said, 'My dream was that the attack came through the skelter instead of – no, I recall more clearly now: as well as by land and sea. While the privateer was temporarily disconnected for the benefit of those who solved the treasure-hunt clues, it would have been easy to send in two or three armed men.'

'Or simply to deliver a powerful bomb,' Mustapha agreed gravely.

'I'm glad I didn't dream that too!' Satamori said, with a nervous chuckle.

Now they had almost reached the skelter; he paused and turned to face his host.

'I am greatly obliged for all your help.'

'There's no need to leave even now if you're not really up to it,' Mustapha said. 'Stay longer, as long as you wish.'

'No, really, I must go. I have work to do, remember. And among the first of my tasks must be to check on what's become of the people who won the treasure-hunt. We are now even shorter of valuable people than we were before. I hope I don't sound cynical, but one must make the best of things.'

'You have a list of some kind?' Mustapha probed.

'One was compiled by Chaim's chief footman, but it was probably destroyed. No matter. I have a good memory, and I was introduced to virtually all of them. I'll start with the recuperator who showed such presence of mind in escaping with the Brazilian girl. Perhaps he's a coward, but the important thing is that he could react so quickly even when he was rather drunk. It shouldn't be hard to locate him; he's bound to show up some time at a public skelter, even if he doesn't feel much inclined to come forward voluntarily for fear of becoming involved in another disaster like that attack on Chaim's house.'

He sighed heavily.

'Oh, Mustapha, I so often find myself wishing that you'd accept a responsible post! You administer this place so skilfully, so tactfully . . . If anybody alive is developing the aesthetic of government which might replace our outworn ideologies, it must be you.'

118

'I have my roots too deep in the old world to achieve that goal,' Mustapha said. 'I have not yet finished identifying and cleansing away the foul psychological poisons which are the inheritance of us all. Perhaps we shall never succeed, or perhaps your treasure-hunt party, which I've spoken of so scathingly, has already found you the person we need, or perhaps he was among the dead. One cannot tell.'

There was a brief silence; then they embraced and Satamori entered the skelter.

The moment the scientist was gone, Mustapha clapped his hands loudly, and Ali appeared as though materializing from the air.

'Has Dykstra not been found yet?'

'Effendi, we are searching the whole planet! But when he appealed to the police for the use of a secure skelter he slipped through our fingers.'

'He must be found! Dr Satamori is about to turn loose the whole resources of the Skelter Authority to locate him. Before I decided to start selling codes to him, I prepared the most exhaustive dossier I could about his life and habits. There is a recorded summary of it in my safe labeled HD. Bring it to me at once. I must refresh my memory and see whether I have any other clues to his probable behavior.'

When the cassette was delivered to him he dropped it into his own specially modified player-recorder, which had an ultra-fast playback attachment; much practice had made him able to follow speech at up to ten times its original speed. It was only a matter of minutes before he clapped his hands again, this time in high excitement, and issued fresh instructions which impressed Ali mightily.

'The effendi indeed deserves that official rank which Dr Satamori offered,' he said. 'One could almost believe him capable of reading men's secret thoughts.'

'Don't waste time flattering me,' Mustapha snapped. 'Go find out whether I've read his thoughts right!'

Anneliese's dress was not yet nearly dry when by a combination of pidgin-English and gestures Hans located it pegged out along with scores of other and much smaller garments on a pole overhanging a shallow stream that ran past the south side of the refuge. Appealing to a helpful young monk who spoke a little more English than most of the staff obtained him a couple of alternatives: a sort of sarong left behind by a visitor from Sri Lanka, the same size as Anneliese, and a suit of pyjama-like jacket and trousers rather too large, which he seized on eagerly since it would cover her completely and he expected that to be the crucial problem.

To his dismay Anneliese cast a single glance at what he had found and shook her head, wrapping her quilt more tightly around her than ever.

'That is for a man,' she said flatly.

'What? But I don't understand.'

'Perhaps you would not have thought of it. I know many women do go around in trousers. But I have always been taught that it is sinful for women to wear men's clothes, or men to wear women's.'

'My dear girl, surely – !'

'Hans, I'm sorry, but I want my dress. It is decently long and it's proper women's clothing. Surely if we have to wait a little while longer, until it's completely dry, that won't matter very much?'

Defeated, Hans turned away. 'I'll see if I can find something else,' he muttered.

'It's not very likely.'

'What?'

'I have been looking through the window.' She blushed brilliant red as she spoke. 'I've seen people walking about as shameless as animals! I shall never do that – never, never!'

Her jaw set stubbornly. For a long moment he gazed at her in disbelief, and then he went out.

Another search of the refuge's clothing store proved even more fruitless than the first; as the young man explained apologetically, lightweight clothing was ordinarily converted into cleaning rags or bandages, while what winter wear was kept – shut at present in closets with branches of pennyroyal and other herbs to discourage moth – would run foul of Anneliese's prejudice against trousers. What more sensible garb, though, for one traveling to a colder climate?

'Is the girl unwell in her mind?' the monk asked at length.

'You might say so,' Hans snapped, and explained about
120

her upbringing. The young man's mouth rounded in amazement.

'I have heard of that. Now I see it, I realize it is even sadder than I was told. Well, we shall just have to find a quick means to dry her dress, if she will put on nothing else and won't go about naked. Perhaps in the kitchens. I shall take care of it.'

Hans muttered a mechanical word of thanks and wandered fretfully away, intending to rejoin Anneliese and see if he could cajole her into a more reasonable attitude.

As he rounded the corner of the corridor leading to her room, however, he heard his name called. Turning, he found the elderly nun whom he had met before hurrying toward him.

'There is friend to see you,' she said, beaming.

'What?'

'At the skelter. All monks and nuns try finding you in all places since half-hour. Has message for you, he say, from mostly famous poet Mustapha Sharif! And is own name of Muley Hassan.'

For an instant the world spun crazily around Hans; then he heard his voice cry, 'He's lying! I don't know anybody called that!'

The nun stared at him, puzzled.

'Is strange, then. He ask by name for you, also for girl. Is – ah – *An-nah-li-zah*, true? An-nah-li-zah Sen-keh!' She looked pleased at having produced the European name in recognizable form.

'Send him away!'

'But he ask by name and – '

'Send him away! Or get me and Anneliese away! Anything so long as you don't tell him where I am!'

'But why, brother? Why this man so make you fear?'

Hans drew a deep breath, and appealed to the one argument he was fairly sure might provoke results.

'Do you wish a man to be murdered here at this refuge? If you don't, you'll do as I say!'

'Murder!' The nun's eyes grew wide in horror. 'He is come to kill you? Oh, then you *must* be sent away!'

Once I met a man
who every day
went around the planet counterclockwise.
He said by this means
he gained a day
and would therefore live for ever.
Unluckily for him
Death measures time
otherwise than with clocks and watches.

— MUSTAPHA SHARIF

Chapter 18

'Hans, what in the world – ?'

'Here's your dress! Put it on, since you won't wear anything else! *Hurry!* Someone's followed us here and we've got to get away!'

He threw the still-damp garment at her; she caught it and clutched it to her bosom, staring wide-eyed not only at him but at the monk and nun who had also come to the door of her room, looking much disturbed at the fact of having to lie. Muley Hassan had been sent to the farthest corner of the refuge on the pretext that Hans had last been reported there; a few precious minutes had been gained, but only Hans's intense assurance that his life was at stake had won that reprieve. It was a cardinal tenet of the Way of Life always to believe that everybody told the truth. Prince Knud had laid that down, at the very beginning, because he said – and with much justice – that the doom of the old world was inherent in its habit of hypocrisy, clear through from bluff in international relations to hard-sell exaggeration in advertising. And because his teachings were so much akin to oriental tradition, they had taken deep root among people like these, on the fringes of the greatest disaster in all of history, who were still even now hunting for clues to help them understand why the population crash called the Blowup had occurred.

Hence the existence of Way of Life refuges like this one all over Asia and Africa and the Pacific . . . and their absence in Europe and North America, places where not only was there no need to explain the causes of the Blowup, but so much damage had been done to the minds of the survivors that the notion of having strangers wander at will among them was untenable.

Praise be for the childlike naïveté of that attitude. Without it . . .

'Do as I say!' Hans roared at Anneliese, and she flinched.

'I am to get dressed with so many people staring?'

No, no, it simply couldn't be possible. It couldn't be that he, Hans Dykstra, was condemned because a stupid girl was ashamed to show her nipples and her crotch . . . But he gathered his wits and without a word rushed the others from the room, catching them by the hands. Over his shoulder he cried, 'Hurry! Hurry!'

And she didn't. Time leaked away while he and the monk and the nun stood irresolute in the corridor, and then another monk came into sight and called something in which Hans was able to detect the name of Muley Hassan, and his patience would endure no longer. He again flung wide the door of Anneliese's room and found her red-faced and struggling to fasten her long drab dress.

'What are you *playing* at?' he demanded.

She exclaimed in horror at having him intrude when she was incompletely covered. Over her bosom, the front-closing zipper was jammed at a height which most girls would regard as excessively modest, but she by contrast covered with both hands.

'It's shrunk and I can't do it up!'

The world turned red, like the fire he had set at the Eriksson house and never seen but could imagine. He seized her by the arm and literally dragged her from the room in disregard of her shrieks of protest. The nun and the two monks tried to interfere, and he brushed them aside and physically carried Anneliese the last few meters to the skelter – and shoved her into it – and punched the first remote code that came to his mind, in Panama.

To the girl, very close to her ear, he said between his teeth, 'You would rather be beaten up, maybe killed, maybe *raped*, than let me see a patch of your chest? Are you insane?'

She fought him for another few seconds, and then wilted against his shoulder, weeping as he pushed her out of the skelter. Here, as almost everywhere, the concourse around the skelter outlets was full of stucks and bracees, making shift to earn their living as touts and shills and guides.

'I don't understand your world!' Anneliese was moaning. 'I hate it – and it makes me terrified!'

Alertly dozens of the watchers reacted, and closed in.

'Ah, sir!' the first said, choosing English – he was a boy of no more than fifteen, but muscular and agile as an eel so that he slipped through the throng. 'You want private place finish raping virgin girl, yes? I got good place cheap, I –'

Hans cuffed him aside with the flat of his hand and looked desperately for a way past the others, but failed to find one. The universe seemed to be full of greedy outstretched hands, shouting mouths, the glint of light on those bracelets which forbade entrance to the skelter system . . .

'Hey, you!'

A booming voice that overrode the clamor from the touts and shills, and a ring of authority that caused them to fall back and give passage to the speaker: a heavy-set man in his early forties, well-dressed, clean-shaven, cast from a different mold. He carried in his left hand a white card that might have been a photograph because he glanced at it before continuing to Hans.

'Aren't you Hans Dykstra? I have a message for you from –'

But already Hans's fevered mind had completed the sentence, by way of an instantaneous detour that posed the question: how did Mustapha manage to ensure that one of his agents was here, in Panama the place I chose at random?

'Quick!' he forced out, and taking Anneliese by the arm again dragged her back into the skelter and punched for . . .

Spitzbergen. (How many more codes can I think of before I

124

have to consult a directory? Before I start accidentally using ones which belong to friends, colleagues at work? Oh, if there were a God I'd pray, I'd pray but there's only the impersonal force that evolved us from the slime . . . !)

'Hans, Hans, let me go!' Anneliese was shrieking, trying to pummel him with her free hand.

The cry attracted attention. Here, in an Arctic winter, the concourse was nearly deserted; those whom chance had stranded this far north spent the time of sunlessness, or so he had been told, adapting the ancient Eskimo practice of wife-swapping to the tenets of the Way of Life. But a fat ugly woman wearing some sort of police-like uniform jumped up from a bench and came toward them, grinning from ear to ear.

'Hey, you're Dykstra, aren't you? I never expected you to –'

And back into the skelter, straight away. Code: Victoria, Vancouver Island, on that western fringe of Canada which had escaped the worst of the fallout from the Blowup.

It was as though Mustapha had multiplied himself, become a sort of all-knowing deity, able to see the entire planet at a single glance.

And again at Victoria . . . ! How – *how* – could that devil Mustapha have planted his agents at every public skelter outlet? There were thousands, and even if he were to send every last member of his retinue to keep watch surely there couldn't be enough to cover every one!

But yet once more a stranger rose and approached with a smile and uttered his name and he fled as before. Where to this time? Somewhere isolated in the middle of an ocean: Tahiti, the Seychelles . . .

He settled for the latter and they emerged at another Victoria, on the island of Mahé, and here nobody was waiting for them. Almost unable to believe it was true, Hans emerged cautiously on to a near-deserted concourse, seeing broken windows around him, much litter blowing in a breeze, a dark man asleep beside a refreshment stand. Nobody else.

He heaved a vast sigh, and let go Anneliese's arm.

'I'm sorry. I'm most terribly sorry, I really am. But you

saw what happened everywhere else we've been until now, didn't you?'

Rubbing the spot where his fingers had clamped, vise-tight, she said, 'All I saw was that a lot of people recognized you and said they wanted to give you a message. I don't know why you have to run away from them. I wish I'd never said I'd come with you. You seem to be treating me more like – like baggage than a person!'

'But the only people I can think of who might want to hound me are criminals, like the one who burgled my home and then burnt it down!' Hans felt perspiration spring from every inch of his skin.

'You have criminal gangs who can be ready and waiting any place you go, ambushing innocent people even though they can go right round the world in next to no time? Then modern life is even more abominable than I already thought it was!'

She gave him a defiant glare, her chin jutted at a sullen angle. His heart sank. Searching for some fragment of consolation, he could find nothing better than the fact that for the moment at least she had forgotten about her stuck zipper.

He soothed her by degrees, until she relaxed enough to agree to accompany him from the concourse and find a place to lodge. The sound of their altercation had awakened the man at the refreshment stand, and he stood up, rubbing sleep from his eyes, and offered his wares: stale-looking pasties and flyblown fruit, old bottles refilled with sickly-looking soft drinks colored repulsively bright red, green and purple.

Hans refused, but asked if there were a hotel to be found ... without much hope.

The man shook his head. 'No, sir. Is not hotels here any more. But is a lodging-house I know, good cheap clean. Is my sister-in-law who runs it. I write address and give directions too.'

He seized a stub of pencil and tore the corner off a yellow sheet of newspaper, and in slow awkward capitals wrote two hard-to-decipher lines. After going through the data with him, Hans thanked him and was about to take Anneliese's arm again when he realized that the man was holding out his palm with a look of annoyance.

Oh. Of course, a tip. He felt in his pocket and produced

126

a couple of coins, suddenly remembering with a wrenching sensation that he had almost no money on him. He had forgotten to pick up his spare cash when he last called by at home.

So he'd have to go back yet one more time, and if there was one place where Mustapha would beyond doubt have planted his agents, it would be at Valletta. It wouldn't be possible for him to get past the privateer and Hans's own skelter, but of course the house still had ordinary doors and windows . . . No, wait a second; hadn't Vanzetti promised that the police would keep a watch on his home? So it would probably be safe to go there after all. And if it proved to be otherwise, then there were alternatives: he could for example go to Recuperation Service headquarters and draw some money there, payment in advance for the compassionate leave he'd applied for. He breathed a little more easily as he led Anneliese out of the concourse building, along a littered street past shabby houses, to another even shabbier one which was obviously the 'good cheap clean' lodging house.

The woman who came to answer Hans's knock at the rickety front door smiled and bobbed and escorted them indoors, explaining that yes, very luckily there was room for someone else because one of the long-term lodgers had just died and nobody had yet rented the room again. She showed them into an ill-furnished cramped room with a double bed, a wash-stand so ancient that had he come on it in the course of his work Hans would have thought it worth recuperating and selling as an antique, and a big wardrobe standing lopsided against the wall because one of its legs was missing.

Anneliese stared about her in dismay. Thinking that it was because of the state of the room, Hans began apologetically to explain about the collapse of the hotel business the world over, so that in most places one could find nothing better than this sort of squalid accommodation, used by stucks and bracees and other poverty-stricken social débris . . . but that wasn't what was on her mind.

'There must be two rooms!' she ordered. 'Find a place where there are two rooms! I will not accept this – we are not married!'

127

And before he could conjure up an answer she was storming at him, a flood of unleashed words that battered his ears until his skull seemed to be ringing like a bell.

'Every man I have met since I came from Brazil is the same, and you too when I thought you were more honest, more *moral!* I was a fool to believe your lies, and I should have known better! All you can think of is your filthy sinful lust, and any way you can cheat a girl, deceive her, force her into a corner she can't escape from, that's what you do! I said I'd come with you because you promised to show me the beautiful side of the modern world, places where people are happy and kind and life is sweet, and what have I seen? What have you brought me to? A horrible shabby filthy *stinking* townful of slums, that's what! Get me away from here *this minute*, and this time *show me what you promised!*'

Many people sit at home
  gnawing their nails,
unable to decide where to go.

An ass – claimed Buridan –
  starved to death
equidistant between bales of hay.

Buridan however was human.
  Other creatures
aren't really as stupid as mankind.

— MUSTAPHA SHARIF

Chapter 19

All his castles in the air were collapsing around Hans now.
He could barely believe that so short a time had transformed
Anneliese from the shy, seemingly affectionate child who
had been so delighted to find someone at Aleuker's whom
she could talk to – albeit slowly and with many verbal foot-
notes – in her own language. Now she seemed to have turned
into a thoroughgoing virago, tongue-lashing him with more
imagination and more sheer anger than Dany had ever
achieved.

Could this be the fruit of the ideals to which she had
been raised? It seemed incredible. How could people get on
with one another if they thought this attitude the right and
proper one?

And then he remembered sickly: they hadn't got on with
one another. They had been so crazy, they had invented
weapons capable of wiping out whole cities-full of people
at a blow, and they had used the skelter first of all to commit
theft, murder and sabotage.

Dazed, there was nothing he could do except comply with
Anneliese's demands. Walking back to the skelter concourse,

129

to the accompaniment of her sniffs and snorts of contempt at the state of this run-down dirty little town which were impervious to all his attempts to interrupt, he searched his mind for somewhere else he might risk taking her.

Tahiti had crossed his mind a little while ago, he recalled. Would that be tolerable by her standards . . . ? Very likely not, because it was a clean smart place patronized by skelter-tourists, people taking long vacations with plenty of money in their pockets. If Anneliese had been horrified to see people going about at the Balinese refuge clad only in kilts and baldrics, even though the costume was practical and they were carrying out their daily tasks, how much more offended would she be at the sight of women and gay men sprawling naked on the beach out of narcissism and the hope that they would attract partners for the night?

He didn't know. He literally had no idea. He couldn't get hold of these lunatic standards which she lived by.

Was there any skelter-using community, anywhere on the planet, conservative enough to satisfy her? Well, if there were it would have to be in Australia. It wasn't that no one at all nowadays adhered to the same sort of principles; it was that those communities where they were in force were disdainful of the skelter, or terrified of it, and he'd never been to any of them apart from making a brief tour of the town near Mustapha's home . . . during which so many people had made signs at him to ward off the Evil Eye, or spat at the prints he left in the dust, that he'd lost count in a few minutes.

Did he know the code for any place in Australia? The answer was no. He'd have to consult a directory, and pick somewhere at random.

There were a few more people in the concourse now, half a dozen altogether including a couple of curious children buying soft drinks at the refreshment stand. He waited until they had been served, then asked about a directory. Recognizing him, the salesman's face fell.

'You did not like the home of my sister-in-law?'

'She – she had only one room, and we wanted two!'

A pause, during which the salesman looked him over with mingled amazement and contempt: if a man can persuade a girl so pretty to travel with him, how can he not share her bed? A good question . . . But he moved at last, pointing toward a booth which Hans had not noticed on the far side of the concourse, and said there was a directory there.

He expected Anneliese to come with him; she declined, and sat down firmly on a vacant bench.

'You make me walk too much! My feet hurt! And this is the world where they told me you never need to walk because you have the skelter!'

So Hans went to the directory booth alone, and leafed through a tattered out-of-date volume with many pages missing. The purpose they had been put to was plain from the stench that arose from a corner of the booth; the floor had subsided, there was a hole in it, and people had used it as an impromptu latrine.

Half-deafened by the buzz of flies that circled that spot, Hans eventually located and memorized the code for the public skelter outlet in Alice Springs, Australia, which – so he seemed to remember – was currently flourishing and certainly must be as conservative as most of the subcontinent. He headed, sighing, back toward the bench where he had left Anneliese . . . and realized with a shock of horror that she wasn't there.

Staring frantically around, he spotted her approaching the skelters, talking animatedly to a man in neatly tailored clothes who certainly had not been on the concourse a few minutes ago.

He shouted at her. Glancing fearfully at him, she clutched her new companion's arm and whispered something that impelled him to hurry her into the nearest booth. Before Hans could catch up, a wash of bright blue light signaled their departure.

To anywhere.

For a long while Hans simply stood there cursing, his hands clenched so tight he fancied blood would run from the tips of his nails. The children regarded him in amazement, sucking their soft drinks noisely through straws; also the other people present gazed at him.

At long last he managed to gather his wits, and said to the air, 'He's not going to get away with it! I'll see him in hell first!'

131

He strode to the same skelter by which Anneliese and the unknown man had traveled, and punched a code he had only used once before but remembered almost better than his own.

It belonged to Mustapha Sharif.

'He has come, effendi,' said Ali, and stood aside from the doorway of the Room of Leopards so that Hans could pass him, shouting wildly.

'What have you done with her, damn you?'

Mustapha, seated cross-legged on a pile of soft cushions, raised the brow over one sightless eye: what do you mean?

'Hans, good day to you,' he murmured. 'I have been half-expecting you . . . Be seated, and let Ali serve you some refreshment.'

'I want to know what you've done with Anneliese!' Hans bellowed.

'You have become separated from her?' Mustapha countered.

'Lost her, as you damned well know!'

'To be strictly accurate, I didn't know. But I'm glad. That is as it ought to be.'

'You . . . ' Hans's voice failed him; he recovered it with a tremendous effort. 'You have the gall to sit there and say she didn't go off with one of your agents?'

'My dear fellow, am I a miracle-worker?'

Bewildered, Hans wondered if he were losing his sanity. Had he not himself found it hard to believe that Mustapha could have his servants ready and waiting at every public skelter on earth? And yet –

'You're not denying you sent your chief scribe Muley in search of me?'

'Indeed not, and in fact he's on his way to join us. I just heard the scuffle of his shoes at the end of the corridor. He almost caught up with you, twice I believe, and I'm very puzzled, not to say offended, at the fact that you decided to avoid him. You made things even worse, I gather, by lying in order to persuade the monks and nuns at the Balinese Way of Life refuge to lie too. Ever since our first meeting you've claimed to follow that Way. It is sad to

132

realize that a friend of long standing has been telling you untruths, isn't it?'

Giddy, Hans had to sit down; the alert Ali made sure that a stool was ready behind his legs.

'But if Anneliese didn't go off with someone you sent after us . . . '

Muley entered silently; Mustapha acknowledged his bow with a brief nod.

'Explain the circumstances,' he invited Hans. And, having heard Hans's broken summary, had to chuckle.

'Oh, Hans, Hans, I suppose I should feel flattered because you thought all that was my doing!'

'Whose, then?' Hans demanded furiously.

'Who but a senior official of the Skelter Authority could ensure that watch was being kept, world-wide, for a single man? Frederick Satamori was here, recovering from the injuries he suffered at Chaim Aleuker's, during the very time when you and I were talking at the house in Sweden: that conversation which you ended in such an unceremonious fashion.' Mustapha had discarded his bandage, but now he raised one hand to part his hair and display a piece of bright pink sticking-plaster covering his scalp-wound from the poker.

'But . . . but Anneliese wouldn't have gone off with a total stranger, even if he is an employee of the Skelter Authority!'

'What grounds do you have to say that she would not?' Mustapha retorted. 'During the few brief hours of your acquaintance at Aleuker's party, had you become such old intimate friends . . . ? No, on the contrary: I say you have one hundred per cent evidence that that's exactly what she would do. Have you not realized, even now, that she is deranged?'

'I – ' Hans's jaw dropped.

'I discern that you had begun to suspect, and were denying the truth to yourself.'

With renewed fury: 'So you told Satamori to find me and Anneliese! Is he pimping for you now? You want her for yourself, is that it? Well, I can tell you – '

'Never in my entire life, and I'm no longer a young man,' Mustapha said thinly, 'have I been so mortally insulted. And I am not the only one to take offense. Look at my servants. Can you not read in their faces that they would cheerfully seize you and drag you screaming up my tallest minaret and pitch you to your death on the flagstones below? It is as gentle a fate as you deserve. But you are yourself insane now. Possibly you always have been. In that case I am myself to blame for having be-friended you. So I will answer with fair words. No, I did not set Satamori on your trail. Owing to the loss of Chaim and other crucial people, he was eager to track down those who had solved the treasure-hunt clues and you were the first person to do so and he wanted to get in touch with you and offer you a better job, more respon-sible, better paid. Instead, you let yourself become obsessed with a mentally-disturbed girl, barely more than a child; you let your wife sacrifice herself and gave perjured evidence about her death; you – '

'Lies, lies!' Hans shrieked.

'Ali, serve our visitor a tranquilizing draught. It will soften his panic and enable him to think and talk more like his normal self.'

Prompt, Ali proffered an engraved brass cup. Hans swept it aside, crying, 'Out to poison me now, are you?'

'Ali, fill two cups; the strain is telling on me and I too would welcome some of that drink. If you choose which cup I should take, will that content you?' Mustapha added to Hans.

Hans licked lips gone suddenly dry. Eventually he nodded.

'Good. I might say: just as well. Because if I had to kill you, I would. I had your predecessor killed when he started pilfering things from the houses we visited together. I do not wish to wear a bracelet . . .

'But I do wish to make several things clear to you, and when your mind is settled enough to take them in, I shall continue with my explanations. I would rather convince you than have your death on my conscience.'

134

I have noticed
how deep in litter is the world.

It is because
nobody cares about anywhere now.

I don't live here!
– they say, and take the skelter.

But they do.
They do live here. This is Earth.

– MUSTAPHA SHARIF

Chapter 20

Perhaps Mustapha was more accustomed to whatever was in the tranquilizing draught; at any rate, he seemed unaffected by it when he had drained his cupful. By contrast Hans was pervaded by sudden alarming detachment, as though his ego had separated from his body and now floated above his head, observing himself, controlling his movement and speech but from a distance, puppet-fashion.

He said, enunciating carefully, 'Well – explanations! And I warn you: make them good ones . . . ' A yawn unexpectedly stretched that last word, and he converted it into a gasp.

Mustapha, apparently not having noticed, said, 'You must have wondered what it is I obtain from visiting abandoned homes with you.'

'Yes, often.'

'I obtain insight into the process that led to my being blinded.'

'How – how . . . ? No, I shouldn't ask. It's too personal.'

'On the contrary; you should have asked long ago, and you would have made more sense of your life. I was blinded because I was looking directly toward a nuclear fireball. It was the bomb that destroyed the Suez Canal. It doesn't matter by whom it was fired. But its glare was focused straight through my corneas, which are as you have seen unmarred, and on each of my retinas the point at which the optic nerve sets in was cicatrized, converted in a fraction of a second to useless scar-tissue. It is because of that experience that when I go to an abandoned home belonging to people who lived by the old standards, I find something different there from what you find. I find a distillation of what they used to disguise the cruelty and brutality they were capable of. You go to such places in a spirit of envy and resentment. You wish you could have lived as they did, not realizing that it would mean paying the spiritual price they paid. At heart you *belong* to that old cruel world.'

'No, no!'

'Do you not? Do you really not? Because I do!'

Confused, Hans shook his head; the sensation was like twitching marionette-strings.

'I belong so completely to that old world, despite all my efforts to identify the foul poisons it has left in the collective psyche of mankind, that when I heard Satamori was going to search for you I gave way to panic. I could foresee you betraying me. It was not until I sent for and re-heard a tape I once compiled about you, the one which documented your past history and impelled me to decide that you and I would become partners in crime, that I realized how stupid I was being. At first I was thinking of catching you and tying you up, as you did me only better – you made a terribly clumsy job of those bonds, you know! Then later I realized that was betraying my own vision of man's ultimate nature . . . and in the upshot, I'm delighted to say, my better judgment has been proven right. You did come here of your own free will; you have become separated from Anneliese to whom as I told you only harm could come from your relationship – '

'Stop, stop! That isn't true!'

'Ah, but it is. Think hard, Hans.' Mustapha leaned forward, his sightless gaze seeming to bore through into Hans's very brain. 'Think first about your own situation. Do you feel the world has treated you unjustly?'

'Yes, damn it, *yes*!' Hans felt tears start to his eyes.

'I haven't done any real harm to anybody, I just got taken aback and miscalculated about a couple of things. It isn't fair that I should have been punished for –'

'Who punished you?' Mustapha slipped in the question with the neatness of a hypodermic needle. 'You are guilty of a major crime, as the standards of today measure crime. You're a code-breaker. So am I.'

'But I only did that because I wanted to get to grips with the past, document it, leave my reports for the archeologists of the future –'

'Not true. If that had been the truth, could you not have gone to your superiors and said that in addition to working as a recuperator, a legal scavenger, you wanted – in your own time – to garner information too? They would never have accorded me that privilege. But to you, a trustworthy and indeed a respected colleague, they would have said yes. You could have had discontinued codes with full legal authority. But you didn't want that. You wanted to be regarded, albeit after your death, as a man who dared to defy society's rules!'

'No, that's not so! They would never have let me – '

'Damnation, man! You met the people, or some of them, who are running Earth these days. You met Satamori and Aleuker and Pech and the others at that ridiculous party! For all I maintain that they're going about saving mankind the wrong way, inventing new rules and regulations when what we most desperately need is to apply common sense instead of inflexible principles that become out of date in a year or two – for all the disagreements I've had with them, I have to concede them this much: they're the most open-minded people ever to achieve such power in the whole of human history. You don't know what Satamori said when he mentioned that he was going to track you down, so I'll tell you. He said, approximately, that it wouldn't matter if you proved to be a coward, as was suggested by the speed of your flight from Chaim's home. What counted was that you were plainly a quick thinker.'

A faint moan escaped from Hans's lips. He tried to stop it, and could not.

His voice colored by pity, Mustapha went on more softly,

'There's one thing you still have to accept, my friend. You are acting as though you became the – the proprietor of this girl Anneliese. You could never have done so. You could at best have been her ... keeper.'

'But she didn't seem to be mentally disturbed!'

'No more do you, from most people's standpoint. Less than – ' Sensing that Hans was drawing breath to interrupt, Mustapha raised one hand to forestall him. 'Less than I do, was what I was about to say. I know for a fact that Chaim Aleuker believed me to be a terribly dangerous man. He suspected me of vaulting ambition, of a lust for power, of degrees of hypocrisy unparalleled in the worst of the olden days ... and with respect to his memory, I must argue that he was wrong.

'Honestly, my friend, how could you imagine that someone in Anneliese's plight could be less than seriously deranged? Your wife Dany, unlikable perhaps, but capable of functioning as a person, more or less, capable of making her own friends and even of being singled out as a recipient of one of those silly treasure-hunt invitations – surely with her before you as an example of how deeply deformed a personality can become thanks to the trauma mankind has undergone, you ought to have seen how much more seriously Anneliese must have been affected? *A priori!* And in addition ... ' Mustapha's voice dropped. 'In addition you *ought* to have applied the same lesson to yourself.'

Hans gulped air, but could not answer.

'So far as I'm concerned,' Mustapha went on, 'I am ashamed of what the old world did to me, and I want the world to know that I'm ashamed. I'm ashamed that there was so much greed and envy, and that greed and envy are in my nature too. I'm ashamed that people had power without responsibility, and since I have power I strive to act in a responsible manner, not by accepting government posts but by listening when those in need come to me, by helping those who cannot help themselves, by admiring the petty achievements of those who have no better and yet do not deserve to have nothing at all ... Possibly I am respected; I believe I am. But that is by strangers, people far away whose only contact with me is through what I have written. What counts above all for me is that I know I am liked by the people who live in the town just beyond the far wall of my home!' He thrust out one chubby arm and slapped what happened to be the head of one of the painted leopards, bowed to the gutting of a deer.

'It is because those who had far more than I dare ever dream of having,' he concluded, 'chose to use their wealth in such abominable ways, that I would rather be regarded as eccentric than join the ruling élite. But that is my personal opinion. I have no right to instruct you to follow my example. What I, or any other man, may justly do is say this to you: you have misjudged yourself, taken the wrong measure of yourself. As a result you have a death on your conscience, and your wife's at that. You have a talent, and from that flows your chance to atone. You dreamed of making the girl Anneliese subservient to you by trapping her in a web of cajolement – but I went over that, and you answered me with a blow on the head. Instead, go to Satamori, accept whatever post he feels you are capable of taking on, dedicate yourself to it. Convert, transform, sublimate your desire for power into liking for work well done. It is possible. I think that what persuaded me to select you as – I use the phrase again – my partner in crime must have been that I sensed your ability to achieve that kind of sublimation. Now prove me right.'

Out of all that long discourse, Hans clutched at and retained one key suggestion. Rising, his mind foggy, he said, 'You want me to go straight to Satamori.'

'I think it is a wise course of action.'

'Very well. Ali, lead me to the nearest skelter and find the code for the headquarters of the Skelter Authority.'

Less than five minutes later he was there. And a young man appeared to him from another skelter after a safe interval, and faced him through armour-glass from behind a reception desk which – Hans didn't have to be told – concealed guns. The pattern was the same at that point in Recuperation HQ which had to be open to the public. When the arrival signal sounded, what had entered the room might not be a person, but a saboteur's bomb.

139

He identified himself, and added, 'I gather Dr Satamori has been looking for me.'

The young man's face brightened.

'I'll say he has! I never before had to issue so many copies of a single person's picture. We've been standing by at every public skelter outlet to try and locate you, but I guess you haven't felt much inclined to travel, hm? I heard the sad news about your wife – if you don't mind my mentioning that? Some people do mind, some don't. Seems to be culturally dependent . . . Well, what can we do for you?'

'Show me to Dr Satamori, I guess,' Hans muttered.

'Well, right this minute he's not here,' the young man said. 'You maybe heard Dr Pech of the Advancement Authority is still hospitalized as a result of what happened at Chaim Aleuker's?'

'I was there!'

'Never! So that's how you met the chief! Well, well! Ah – as I was saying, Dr Satamori has gone to call on Dr Pech in the hospital, but if you'd care to wait he said he wouldn't be long, maybe another twenty minutes at most, or if you'd prefer to come back, or have him call you . . . ?'

A vast weariness was pervading Hans's mind now. The echo of the advice he had been given by Mustapha was fading away, as though the effect of the tranquilizing drink had muted the impact of the words. Overlaying it now were deep, deep emotions: disappointment, frustration, horror . . . He said gruffly, 'No, I guess I'd rather not wait. But if you can give me a piece of paper and an envelope, I'd like to leave a note.'

'Surely! Here you are!'

He sat down, wrote the note – no more than ten lines – and re-read it, and sealed the envelope and handed it over. Then he headed for the skelter without another word.

'Hey!' the young man said, and then much louder and far more urgently, 'Hey! That's not – !'

He had a clear sight of the nine-digit code Hans was punching. And it was not one which you'd expect a traveler to select.

'I tried to stop him – shouted out, even before he finished composing all nine digits!' the young man mourned. 'One gets into the habit of automatically glancing at what people are punching, just in case –'

'Stop blaming yourself,' Satamori said glacially, seated at his desk and reading for the third or fourth time the note which Hans had left. 'You weren't to know in advance he was punching the code for an incinerator.'

He glanced at the skelter in the corner of his own office, and could not repress a shudder.

'That will be all,' he added, and the young man went out, shaking his head as automatically as a porcelain mandarin.

Alone, Satamori stared at the note and tried to consult in his mind with Chaim Aleuker, with Boris Pech, with the miserable girl whom his agents had luckily caught up with in – of all places – the Seychelles, and who would probably be fit to take her place in society in a few years' time, after treatment by Karl Bonetti. He fancied he could hear all their voices, blended into a single voice, inside his head. They agreed, they concurred, they were unanimous.

The note said that Mustapha Sharif had for years been guilty of selling illegal codes to abandoned houses. There were several of the actual codes listed.

'But I know him,' Satamori said under his breath. 'I respect him. More importantly, I like him, even though we're forever arguing. To see him braced . . . No, it would be – unworthy. Whatever his reasons, I'm sure they were justified. And he's always said, rightly, that we must never put an absolute straitjacket of rules and regulations around the world again. Maybe what brought us to the Blowup was the simple operation of an inflexible natural law. Equally, it might have been the excessive constriction of inflexible man-made laws. Man likes to be free. When he's fettered he gets angry and lashes out.'

He reached his decision. Rising, he walked to his private skelter and tossed the note on to its floor. Then, at the full stretch of his arm, he composed the same nine-digit code which had taken Hans Dykstra on the longest of all journeys so far made possible by the skelter – the longest that ever would be possible, indeed – and the note followed him into eternity.

He returned to his desk. There was as always very much work to be done.

INTERFACE U

You
stood before the skelter
thinking it was new and strange
to confront so many options

You
overlooked the fact
that every dawn since time began
has lighted uncountable choices

— MUSTAPHA SHARIF

NEL BESTSELLERS

Crime

T027 821	GAUDY NIGHT	Dorothy L. Sayers	75p
T030 180	UNNATURAL DEATH	Dorothy L. Sayers	60p
T026 663	THE DOCUMENTS IN THE CASE	Dorothy L. Sayers	50p

Fiction

T029 522	HATTER'S CASTLE	A. J. Cronin	£1.00
T030 199	CRUSADER'S TOMB	A. J. Cronin	£1.25
T031 276	THE CITADEL	A. J. Cronin	95p
T029 158	THE STARS LOOK DOWN	A. J. Cronin	£1.00
T022 021	THREE LOVES	A. J. Cronin	90p
T022 536	THE HARRAD EXPERIMENT	Robert H. Rimmer	50p
T022 994	THE DREAM MERCHANTS	Harold Robbins	95p
T023 303	THE PIRATE	Harold Robbins	95p
T022 986	THE CARPETBAGGERS	Harold Robbins	£1.00
T031 667	WHERE LOVE HAS GONE	Harold Robbins	£1.00
T023 958	THE ADVENTURERS	Harold Robbins	£1.00
T031 659	THE INHERITORS	Harold Robbins	95p
T031 586	STILETTO	Harold Robbins	60p
T025 268	NEVER LEAVE ME	Harold Robbins	50p
T025 292	NEVER LOVE A STRANGER	Harold Robbins	90p
T022 226	A STONE FOR DANNY FISHER	Harold Robbins	80p
T031 640	79 PARK AVENUE	Harold Robbins	80p
T027 945	THE BETSY	Harold Robbins	90p
T031 241	EVENING IN BYZANTIUM	Irwin Shaw	75p
T029 557	RICH MAN, POOR MAN	Irwin Shaw	£1.25

Historical

T023 079	LORD GEOFFREY'S FANCY	Alfred Duggan	60p
T024 903	THE KING OF ATHELNEY	Alfred Duggan	60p
T023 125	FOX 11: FIRESHIP	Adam Hardy	35p
T024 946	FOX 12: BLOOD BEACH	Adam Hardy	35p
T027 651	FOX 13: SEA FLAME	Adam Hardy	40p

Science Fiction

T029 492	STRANGER IN A STRANGE LAND	Robert Heinlein	80p
T029 484	I WILL FEAR NO EVIL	Robert Heinlein	95p
T031 462	DUNE	Frank Herbert	£1.25
T022 854	DUNE MESSIAH	Frank Herbert	60p

War

T027 066	COLDITZ: THE GERMAN STORY	Reinhold Eggers	50p
T025 438	LILLIPUT FLEET	A. Cecil Hampshire	50p
T026 299	TRAWLERS GO TO WAR	Lund & Ludlam	50p

Western

T020 754	EDGE 15: BLOOD RUN	George Gilman	35p
T022 706	EDGE 16: THE FINAL SHOT	George Gilman	35p
T024 881	EDGE 17: VENGEANCE VALLEY	George Gilman	40p

General

T021 009	SEX MANNERS FOR MEN	Robert Chartham	35p
T023 206	THE BOOK OF LOVE	Dr David Delvin	90p
T028 828	THE LONG BANANA SKIN	Michael Bentine	90p

NEL P.O. BOX 11, FALMOUTH TR10 9EN, CORNWALL:

For U.K.: Customers should include to cover postage, 19p for the first book plus 9p per copy for each additional book ordered up to a maximum charge of 73p.

For B.F.P.O. and Eire: Customers should include to cover postage, 19p for the first book plus 9p per copy for the next 6 and thereafter 3p per book.

For Overseas: Customers should include to cover postage, 20p for the first book plus 10p per copy for each additional book.

Name ....

Address...

....

Title ....
(NOVEMBER)

Whilst every effort is made to maintain prices, new editions or printings may carry an increased price and the actual price of the edition supplied will apply.